Bloody Twine #1
Twisted Tales with Twisted Endings
Matthew L. Marlott

Bloody Twine #1
Copyright 1st ed. © 2023 Matthew L. Marlott

ISBN: 979-8-9894444-1-0

This book is for all who just wish to sit back, relax, and enjoy some twisted tales with twisted endings. This book is dedicated to fans of traditional horror.
If you like this book, give it a good review and tell me what your favorite story was in this collection.

Table of Contents

Preface

These stories were originally published on my own personal site, bloodytwine.com. It's a little site that has received an equal amount of little attention, but it's mine, and I'm proud of it. I use this site to perfect my stories, and thanks to it, you have these bundles of fine short horror tales you can now peruse and enjoy at your leisure.

Imagine walking into an abandoned storage room filled with old newspapers and magazines, all articles stacked in bundles neatly tied with twine, but then you discover other bundles, bundles not so neatly tied, ragged bundles of yellowed and partially-charred paper tied in bloodstained twine.

You see, some stories are meant to educate, and some stories are meant to entertain, but some stories…some stories are simply looking for a victim.

Enjoy.

Bloody Twine #1

There's a hidden door in the school.
Mr. Keys was old. He was the perfect target for Lori and her friends, mainly because they had nothing better to do. Tormenting the old man was a welcomed diversion from the ennui and droll of living out a teen's existence, and almost anything was better than dealing with the problems inherent in high school…
Average Read Time: 14m 13s

It's all worth it for the Carter Diamond.
Kara slipped through the now open window, Conner right behind her. This was their one chance to hit it big, now that the power was out across town. That meant the power was out at the old Carter Estate, and that meant the security system was down, too…
Average Read Time: 11m 41s

That painting's a killer work of art.
The painting was of a large wooden ship, an old-timey thing called a "sloop," but that wasn't scary. It was the people on the ship that scared him, because they looked mean, as did their captain, a big man with a black beard and an eyepatch along with a funny black hat. This man looked to be the meanest of them all…
Average Read Time: 12m 43s

What IS under there?

His mother's face was indeed peeling, peeling upon her left cheek, just a little, but enough to bother him, the pale skin off a tiny sliver, a fleck of jet black, like coal, beneath it…
Average Read Time: 6m 44s

She must find the courage to climb.
Eun-Yeong looked past the sprawling meadow outside the house. She looked out toward the row of oak trees growing on the side of the cliff they lived upon. There, leaning against the tallest oak, was their wooden ladder…
Average Read Time: 7m 35s

It's all peripheral.
Dr. Andrew Sidirov walked down the hallway to room 312. The patient in question was one Mr. Maximillian Davies, a former research assistant to the now deceased Professor Angus Macnally…
Average Read Time: 10m 28s

Don't light it.
Denetor waited in the lineup with the other acolytes. Their initiation was about to begin, and they would soon be full-fledged priests of the Seven Lights. Only acolytes were allowed into the recesses of the temple this time of year, that time just before harvest, that time when the guiding spirits were summoned and released into the land for the good will and fortune for all…
Average Read Time: 8m 47s

There's no love lost here.

Their father had passed away not more than a month ago, but the old fool had gotten into more than enough trouble with his creditors, and now the bank had taken almost everything. But Sally knew that the paranoid old man had stashed away some of his cash somewhere within the old mansion, and dollars to donuts, Alice had found it...

Average Read Time: 6m 45s

There will be blood.

Roren stared up at his master, the Great Sage, Althar. They were in the Grand Hall of the Imperial Palace, and many, many people were gathered here. It was due to the fact that Emperor Thardon was dead, assassinated in his bed while he lay asleep...

Average Read Time: 11m 37s

Time for the ol' class fieldtrip.

Today was an exciting day for him, and for everyone else, for that matter. They were finally beginning their fieldtrip to the Yard, a day long in the making. As his friends and fellow classmates boarded the bus right along with him, Jimmy was just happy he didn't have to sit through another boring class. He liked the fun stuff anyway...

Average Read Time: 12m 32s

#1...MR. KEYS

There's a hidden door in the school.

Mr. Keys was old. He was the perfect target for Lori and her friends, mainly because they had nothing better to do. Tormenting the old man was a welcomed diversion from the ennui and droll of living out a teen's existence, and almost anything was better than dealing with the problems inherent in high school.

The old man held a number of keys that jangled from his belt, but there was one in particular that had caught Lori's eye, and that was the large, plain, iron key that crowned the ancient janitor's metal keyring. This thing was a throwback to the very old days, the days when doors were big metal things that took some muscle to open, and there was one such door in the school, though no one went near it.

The door in question was at the back of the boiler room in the basement, so getting in that room was going to take more than one key, but stealing the old man's keyring would not be difficult. It was simply a matter of timing, since the doddering old fool was way past his expiration date, and he fell asleep on the job quite often.

"Why is he even still employed here?" asked Lori, but the others could not give her an answer that made sense.

"Maybe he works for the Mob," said Sasha, but she was a flighty ditz with the working intelligence of your typical squid, so her suggestions were always stupid.

"They probably just feel sorry for him," said Denise, and though Denise was levelheaded, Lori seriously doubted that was the reason why Mr. Keys still worked at the school, or anywhere, for that matter.

"I don't care why he's still here," said Lori. "What I want to know is what's behind that door that supposedly exists in the basement. That key has got to open it…I know it."

"I don't know…" said Denise, but Lori would not hear it.

"Don't be such a wuss," frowned Lori. "Let's just grab that ring right now while he's still in dreamland. The old man's asleep on the job again, and since we have an early out, everyone thinks we've already left the school."

And now was the perfect time to do it. It was a little past one, and the other seniors were walking out to their cars or heading for a bus, so now was the time to have some rare fun in this educational pit others called school. They could all pile into Sasha's car after they'd explored a little anyway.

There was no one else around as they brazenly walked into the janitor's office. The little room was cluttered with all kinds of janitorial crap, and in the middle of that crap was a swivel chair and a desk. In that chair was a sleeping Mr. Keys, his boots up on the desk, the old man snoring away, and in Mr. Keys' left hand was his keyring, and on that keyring was the key in question.

It was a simple thing to pry his fingers loose from the keyring, a simple task that Lori had no trouble in actually performing, and after that minor dose of stress, they left Mr. Keys to his daily nap and quickly went on their way.

"If anyone asks, we're picking up some extra credit," said Lori. "Just be confident and smile, and they'll believe anything."

"Got it," said Denise.

They headed to the first floor of the school to the basement-stairs door. It took virtually no time to get there, but fishing for the right key took some work. Nevertheless, one of the keys fit, so they unlocked that door and journeyed down into an area few other classmates had ever seen.

"This is actually exciting," said Sasha. "I'm actually shivering."

"Let's…Let's just get this over with," said Denise, and Lori could tell that her levelheaded friend was scared.

"You're such a baby," said Lori. "There's probably nothing down here. There probably isn't even a big metal door."

"There is one," said Sasha matter-of-factly. "My cousin, Benny, saw it with Carl Richmond."

"Your cousin, Benny, ate paint chips when he was a kid," frowned Lori. "And Carl Richmond's a giant stoner. He said he saw the face of Jesus in his microwavable burrito down at the Busy All…Oh, I believe there's some kind of door for this key, but not because of some stupid rumor…You know what? Let's just go. I've got exploring to do."

They walked through the basement-floor hall, but it was nothing special. The boiler room, however, was the prize they were looking for, and they found it without too much trouble. It was the very last door at the end of the hall, the door's plain wooden form stacked in shadow, its subtle presence stashed away all by its lonesome.

"Now we see if there is a Santa Claus," grinned Lori as she unlocked the boiler room door.

The first thing they did was flip on the lights. The second thing they did was look around in wide-eyed disgust.

The boiler room was a dusty, cobweb-ridden hole where the school boiler was located, though the rusty thing looked as if it had been made in the late 1800s. Lori wondered how it even functioned at all.

"This is what heats our water?" she asked. "I'm going bottled all the way from now on."

"Isn't that bad for the environment?" asked Sasha.

"So's your waistline, but no one cares about that, either," frowned Lori.

Sasha frowned in return over that obvious insult, but the airhead was also a distraction, so some order had to be handed down.

"Let's just find this so-called door and get out of here," said Denise. "I don't like this place at all."

"Yeah," frowned Lori. "Adventure or not, this place sucks."

They walked past the boiler, past old, wet, moldy, cardboard boxes, past shelves full of old tools and such, but there was only one door at the back of the room, and it was made of wood, not metal.

"This must be it," said Denise.

"This can't be it," scoffed Lori. "There's supposed to be a metal door."

"I know," said Sasha. "I feel robbed."

"So much for your cousin and his hemp buddy," sighed Lori. "Oh, well. Let's open it anyway."

She tried the old brass doorknob before anyone could protest, but the door was shut tight.

"It's locked," frowned Lori. "One of these keys has to open it."

"I don't like this…" warned Denise.

"You don't like anything," replied Lori. "I'm opening it. I want to see what's inside…Besides, it's probably just an old storeroom."

She tried to unlock the door with the large iron key, but it was way too big to fit. Disappointed, she tried the other keys until one of them opened the door, a hassle in itself to find the right key, much like the hassle in finding the key to the door for the actual basement.

The door unlocked with a loud click.

"Bingo," said Lori.

They flipped on the light as they walked into the small room set before them.

Lori took her time studying the small space.

The room was indeed small, but it was not like any other room in the school. The overhead lamp revealed what looked like a small study area, complete with a desk, a swivel chair, and a large memo-board one always saw in those police investigation shows. There was a metal filing cabinet with locked drawers in the corner and a large wooden bookshelf right next to it, that bookshelf lined with a number of old dusty books.

"What have we here?" asked Lori in both amusement and wonder.

"This is not what I was expecting at all," said Denise.

"What is this little room?" asked Sasha.

Lori studied the memo-board on the wall, its rigid paper-tacked form mounted directly above the wooden desk. There were old newspaper clippings, articles of missing persons, many of them, in fact, all tacked upon the board in no seemingly-logical order.

She looked down at the desk and noticed similar articles of old print scattered across its wooden surface.

"This is…" started Denise.

Her voice was shaky, a nervousness beneath the breath that was impossible to ignore.

"Yeah," said Lori quietly. "This is like one of those true-crime serial-killer dens."

"Do you think Mr. Keys is…?" trailed Denise.

"Is what?" asked Sasha in stupid reply.

"A psycho, dummy," frowned Lori. "Look at this stuff. All of these people went missing over the years. Either Mr. Keys has a really weird hobby, or he's a…Wait a minute…"

Something stood out amongst the articles, something that had caught her eye. Even Denise had not noticed it.

"Look," said Lori with a smug grin. "Look at the dates on these. These people all went missing over two years of time…fifty years ago."

"What?" asked Denise. "How do you fig…Oh, my God…You're right."

"Fifty years ago?" asked Sasha. "I can't even imagine that long ago…"

"You can't imagine last week," frowned Lori.

"Stop making fun of me," frowned Sasha in return.

"Then start being useful," replied Lori.

"I am useful," argued Sasha.

"And how is that?" asked Lori.

"Umm…" began Sasha.

"That's what I thought," scowled Lori.

"No, wait," replied Sasha as she cocked her head to one side. "That picture there in the middle of the board. That one has a different year than the others."

"She's right," said Denise. "This one's from January of 1973. The others are dated from over the course of 1971 through 1972. This must be the last missing-persons' listing…"

"That we know of," scoffed Lori. "Here, let me take a look…"

She squinted in the dim electric lighting to read the old newspaper print.

"Amanda Keys, age 30, was reported missing by her husband, Desmond Keys, on January 7th," read Lori. "She was last seen walking through State Road Park after dark, around 8:45 P.M. She is reported to be 5'4", weighing approximately 135 lbs., with dark hair and eyes, and was last seen wearing a dark-blue parka and blue jeans."

"Keys?" asked Denise. "As in Mr. Keys?"

"I wonder if she's his wife?" asked Sasha.

"No, she's not his wife, you dim…" started Lori, but then she thought better about it. "You know…we don't know Mr. Keys' first name, but I bet it's Desmond. Maybe this is his old janitorial room…Maybe…just maybe…he actually *is* a psycho…I bet he murdered all of these people, and then his wife found out about it, and then he offed her, too."

"Or he was obsessed with finding her," shrugged Denise. "She disappeared, and according to these clippings, she was the last one to go missing. I mean, if I were him, and my wife went missing, I'd look for her."

"Ugh, you're no fun," frowned Lori. "I wanted to scare Sasha."

"I…I am scared," stammered Sasha.

"Wow," said Lori. "That was easy."

"N…No," stammered Sasha. "Look at these books, guys!"

"What are you on about?" asked Lori.

Sasha was always finding some way to be stupid, but this time was different. Sasha was peering at the books on the bookshelf, something they had not yet investigated, so Lori pushed her ditzy friend aside to investigate said books on the bookshelf, and the hairs immediately stood up on the back of her neck.

Every book was something on the occult, all in different languages. There were books in Latin, Greek, and some languages Lori had never even heard of. Some of them were extremely old, so old that the bindings were made from leather strips.

"What is all of this?" asked Denise in a shaky voice.

But Lori refused to be scared. She'd come this far, so she wasn't about to turn chicken now.

"So, he is a psycho," she said firmly. "He's probably into some kind of cult or something that sacrifices people to a harvest god or whatever…So, he's a nutjob. We can turn him in, and then we'll all be heroes."

"What?" asked Denise in audible disbelief.

"If we turn in Mr. Keys for murder, we'll be heroes," grinned Lori. "All we need is some solid evidence that he murdered someone, and we have him over a barrel. It's that simple. I mean, this stuff is compelling, but it's not enough. We need something more solid. Something that will stick."

"Like what?" asked Sasha.

"Use your imagination," shrugged Lori. "Look around."

"I don't know about this, Lori," said Denise nervously.

"You never want to have any fun," frowned Lori. "Just look around already."

"What about these metal drawers?" asked Sasha.

"Good idea," replied Lori. "You're on a roll today, Sasha."

"Thanks!" smiled Sasha.

"There might be incriminating evidence in one of these drawers," said Lori.

"Or more information we could use to figure all of this out," said Denise.

"That's what we're doing," sighed Lori. "Stop ruining the suspense, please."

She ignored her practical friend and fished through the keys on the keyring again until she found one small enough to actually fit the filing-cabinet locks.

"Let's see if this one works," she said as she held up the key.

"Try the bottom one first," said Sasha. "The evidence is always in the bottom one in the movies."

Lori gave her the best "Are you stupid?" stare she possibly could before shaking her head in mild disgust. Nevertheless, she bent down and tried the bottom-drawer lock.

There was a loud "CLICK!" as the lock turned over.

"Got it," she said confidently.

She pulled open the drawer, but it would only open part of the way, only a crack to allow in a hand and some of the arm.

"It's stuck," she grunted as she pulled hard on it a couple of times.

Unfortunately, the drawer would not budge.

"It won't open," frowned Lori. "Sasha…reach in there and feel around."

"What?" asked Sasha. "Why me?"

"Because I need Denise's expertise in case you lose an arm," grinned Lori.

"That's not funny, Lori," frowned Denise. "Come on."

"I'm just joking, you rube," sighed Lori in return. "Don't be such a dink…Anyway, it won't open all the way, so that's that. I'm not putting my hand in there. There might be spiders or something crawling around in it."

"I'll do it," said Sasha. "I'm not afraid of spiders."

"Sasha, you don't have to—" started Denise.

"It's okay," said Sasha as she waved her off. "I don't mind."

Lori stood up and stepped out of the way as Sasha bent down and took her place in front of the filing cabinet. The airhead reached into the cabinet with her left arm and felt around.

Her eyes went wide with surprise a second later.

"There's something in here!" she said in excitement. "It feels like some kind of lever!"

"Lever?" asked Lori in disbelief. "What?"

"No, really!" replied Sasha. "It's a lever!...I'm going to pull it."

"Sasha, I don't think that's a good idea…" said Denise, but she was ignored yet again.

Sasha grunted as she pulled hard on the "lever" inside the bottom drawer of the filing cabinet. They all heard another loud "CLICK!," and then the real excitement began.

The wooden bookshelf next to the cabinet groaned and slid on geared wheels as it sidled to its own left, their right. It slid aside to reveal a large black-iron door behind it, that door bedecked with a strange circle of red paint, that painted circle bedecked with its own strange lines and even stranger symbols. Those symbols reeked of the occult, just like the books on the bookshelf that had been hiding the wretched door.

"Oh, my God," whispered Denise in audible fear.

"Big time bingo," smirked Lori. "There it is."

"I told you there was a door," said Sasha as she stood up and brushed herself off.

In the center of the painted circle upon the iron door was a large keyhole, and Lori knew exactly which key to try first.

She held up the large iron key on the keyring and jangled the keys.

"Moment of truth, ladies," she grinned.

"I…I don't like this," stammered Denise. "If Mr. Keys is a psycho, he might have hidden the bodies in there…"

"I know," grinned Lori. "I want to see some corpses, don't you?"

"Lori, wait…" warned Denise.

Lori stuck the key in the lock but did not turn it.

"Now we'll see what's behind door number three…" she started, but she was interrupted by a frantic command.

"STOP!" came a loud voice.

Both Sasha and Denise shrieked at the same time, and even Lori jumped a little at the sudden scare. Her heart leapt into her throat at the sight of old Mr. Keys at the little room's entrance, the old man's face a portrait of borderline panic.

Still, Lori would not be intimidated by the old man.

"You can't open that door!" barked Mr. Keys.

"And why not?" asked Lori. "What are you hiding, old man?...You killed all of those people, didn't you? All of those missing people up on the wall. You murdered them, didn't you?

"No…" said the old man as he shook his head. "No, I didn't…"

"You did, didn't you?" said Lori. "Then you killed your wife when she found out, huh?"

The old man's face crumpled inwardly with some private horror at the mention of his wife.

Lori figured her instincts to be right, so she pressed him on the accusation.

"That's it, isn't it?" she asked. "She's in there, isn't she?"

"You don't understand," choked out the old man. "I left her in that pit to protect everyone. She's evil…"

His confession shocked Lori for a moment, but she quickly got over it. It was clear that Amanda Keys was in the room behind the metal door, and that was all the evidence Lori was looking for.

"So, you did kill her," grinned Lori. "You're just another nutcase…but there're three of us and only one of you…Plus, you're old…Oh, yeah…You've been caught old man. You killed all those people and then killed your wife because of some crazy cultist nonsense. How cliché."

"I didn't kill those people…" said Mr. Keys as he shook his greyed head in vehement denial. "You can't open that door…You don't understand…When I found out why they went missing…when I found out what she was…You can't open that door…She's pure evil…"

"Was, Mr. Keys," frowned Lori. "Was."

She grunted as she twisted the key and felt the tumblers turn over with a dull clanging sound.

"No…" said Mr. Keys in visible wide-eyed terror. "Not was…She still is…"

The old man turned and ran from the room, running from whatever crazed horror was playing out in his deranged mind, and he was far spryer than he appeared to be for his age.

"He's getting away!" cried Denise.

"Let him go," frowned Lori. "He won't get far. We'll report him in a moment, and the police will pick him up after that. Besides…I want to see the body."

"What?" asked both Sasha and Denise at the same time.

But Lori did not give them time to argue. She knew they would only tell her no, so she gripped the short metal handle on the left side of the door, planted her feet, and pulled hard. The huge metal door opened outward with a loud creak as years of rust and dust fell away from it in a small choking cloud.

The three girls stared into a wall of black so pervasive that even the fluorescent lights of the old janitorial room could not penetrate it, a wall of ebony that led into a darkness so pitch that it looked alive.

The hairs on the back of Lori's neck stood up as an absolute chill wafted from the dark before her and reached straight down into her bones.

"What the…?" she whispered in a voice pulled hoarse by the freezing air around her.

She realized her mistake too late as a pair of white bony arms wrapped in the tattered rags of a dark-blue parka, the skin pale and stretched like albino leather on distal twigs, reached forth from the black, and two weirdly long hands with black nails on spindly fingers clutched her shirt and pulled her into the absolute void.

#2...THE BUST OF OLD CARTER

It's all worth it for the Carter Diamond.

Kara slipped through the now open window, Conner right behind her. This was their one chance to hit it big, now that the power was out across town. That meant the power was out at the old Carter Estate, and that meant the security system was down, too.

She had cased the place for some time, and she had known exactly which window to try, one that someone, somewhere, had forgotten to lock. It was the security system that was the real problem, however, as it had been set up to activate upon the opening of any window or exterior door in the house, and it would activate unless the correct code was punched into the alarm system before entering, but that problem was solved for the time being.

There was a storm raging outside, the wind and rain howling as if a fury from the heavens, but that was what they had been counting on. They had both known that the power would eventually go out, and it had, so now was the time to strike.

Kara entered a small room with a few chairs surrounding a circular wooden table, the room itself nothing special, probably a room for drinking tea or whatever it was rich people did with small out-of-the-way rooms, but it was her sluggish partner in crime that was currently holding her attention and not the lack of the room's contents.

"Come on," said Kara. "You're too slow."

"Quiet!" hissed Conner.

"There's no one here," replied Kara. "Besides, everyone knows thieves don't come out in the rain. They only strike on sunny days."

"What?" asked Conner in audible confusion. "That doesn't make any sense."

"It makes perfect sense," said Kara. "Now shut up, and let's find that bust."

"Don't tell me to shut up, you little—" hissed Conner.

Kara actually did shut him up by raising one hand to his face. She heard him suck in his breath in rage, but his tantrums didn't matter. She needed a second person with her for this job, because there was no way she was hitting the Carter Estate alone. Yeah, she couldn't stand Conner half the time, but he was good at spotting things that would otherwise remain hidden, so he was the only natural choice.

Really, all she needed was the bust. The Carter story had been around for as long as she'd been alive, and it was a doozy. Old man Carter was a millionaire back in the day, an eccentric old coot with a fortune to boot, but that money had been spirited away by his family a long time ago. No, it was the Carter Diamond that Kara was interested in, because that was the real fortune of the family.

"All we need is that bust," said Kara.

"So you say," replied Conner.

They had their flashlights out and flipped on, the beams crossing to and fro as they walked from one large room to the next.

The mansion they were exploring was in good condition despite its age; the Carters' three surviving children had taken good care of it, though none of them actually lived here. The surviving Carter siblings were all now in their seventies and eighties, and there was talk of the place becoming a museum once they passed away.

"Mr. Carter obtained one of the largest diamonds in the world from one of his overseas investments," explained Kara. "The Carter Diamond has been missing for…well…since the old coot died."

"So why are we looking for a statue?" asked Conner. "Do you know something?"

"Yeah," said Kara.

"Good, because we could run off with any of this stuff and make some quick cash," said Conner.

"Stop thinking so small," frowned Kara. "That diamond makes this crap look like…uhhh…crap."

"So what's so special about this bust?" asked Conner.

"I was getting to that," said Kara.

They entered a large sitting room and shone the beams on everything they possibly could. Yeah, the flashing lights could probably be seen from outside, but with the storm going on and with the power out…nobody gave a crap right now about the Carter Estate.

"Mrs. Carter was crazy," explained Kara. "She was cold and distant, and her kids described her personality as 'a ruthless piece of wood.' She was, however, an artist and a sculptor, a famous one, and Mr. Carter married her because he liked her art. He got that diamond for her as a wedding gift. Her state of mind and the Carter fortune were the reasons the police immediately suspected her when they found Mr. Carter's body."

"He was murdered, then?" asked Conner.

"Oh, yeah," continued Kara. "I'd say so. When I say they found his body, that's all they found. His head was missing."

"Oof," said Conner. "Sucks to be him."

"Yeah," said Kara. "His head was never found, but neither was the diamond."

"So why are we looking for this bust, then?" asked Conner.

"For the diamond, meathead," said Kara.

"Watch it," warned Conner.

"The diamond was never found," repeated Kara. "Mrs. Carter was committed to an asylum by the state, but she insisted that the bust of her husband was her 'most prized possession.' I'm telling you, that diamond is in the bust."

"You think she hid it in there?" asked Conner.

"Absolutely," nodded Kara. "She was a talented sculptor, and she could have easily hidden the diamond in that bust."

"It's been like, what? Since the '60s?" asked Conner. "Don't you think someone else would have figured this out by now?"

"People are stupid and shortsighted," frowned Kara. "Besides, Mrs. Carter never confessed to the murder of her husband. Even so, she got put in a nut house anyway. Her story, combined with the way Mr. Carter died…"

"Beheading," nodded Conner.

"Right," continued Kara. "That stuff took the forefront. No one even thought about the bust in relation to the diamond. All we have to do is find the bust and nab it. Then it's all good."

"And what if it's just a bust?" asked Conner. "What then?"

"Then we grab some stuff and make some quick cash," shrugged Kara. "It's a win-win."

"Makes sense to me," said Conner. "Let's find this bust, then."

They walked down a hall with red wallpaper, shined their lights in several small rooms, and found several busts and statuary in general, but nothing resembling old Mr. Carter.

Kara sucked in her breath as she felt Conner's fingers dig into her right shoulder from behind.

"Wait, stop!" hissed Conner. "Did you see that?"

"See what?" asked Kara in irritation.

She turned to look at Conner's face in the dim glow of their flashlights. The young man was suddenly shaken, an aura of tangible fear surrounding him.

"Where did Mrs. Carter die?" he asked.

"What?" asked Kara. "She died here after she was released from the asylum…Why?"

"I saw her," said Conner in a shaky voice.

"You saw the ghost of old Mrs. Carter?" asked Kara in disbelief.

"Y…Yeah…" stammered Conner.

"That's bull—" started Kara.

She sensed a presence from a nearby room, swiveled, and saw the tail end of the hem of a black dress trail along the floor.

"What the…!" exclaimed Kara. "Who's there!"

They both turned at the same time to shine their lights upon a sliver of shadow at the end of the hall. There, at the end of the hall, was the figure of an old woman in a black dress, her hair white with age, her wrinkled face covered by a black veil.

Kara felt her blood shoot straight through her veins as the lights landed upon the old woman. Even worse, the woman in the black dress vanished into thin air when the lights lingered upon her, her morose profile vanishing as if she had never existed at all.

"That's it!" cried Conner. "I'm getting out of here!"

But this was not the answer Kara wanted to hear. She had come for the crown jewel of the Carter fortune, and she was not leaving without it. Come Hell or highwater, she was not giving in to some specter from beyond the grave.

"No, you're not!" hissed Kara. "Ghost or not, I'm not leaving without that diamond! Now, you're going to man up and help me carry that bust! The storm's still raging, the power's still out, and this is the only chance we're going to get!"

"B…But the ghost…" whined Conner.

"Doesn't matter," growled Kara. "I want that diamond, Conner. I'm not leaving without it. I'm not letting some crazy old dead woman stop me, either…Besides, have you ever heard of a ghost killing someone? Like legitimately?"

"N…No…" said Conner in a shaky voice.

"Good," frowned Kara. "Now pull up your big-boy pants and help me find that bust."

They walked down the hall and entered a large room, the dining room by the looks of the long rectangular table in the center of it.

The dining-room table was surrounded by a number of well-taken-care-of wooden chairs. There were a couple of unlit candles on the table, long white things in silver holders, but other than that, the decoration in the room was pretty sparse.

"Not in here, either," whispered Kara.

The candles upon the table lit by themselves, and Conner shrieked as he gripped Kara's shoulders from behind.

"Will you quit that!" hissed Kara. "So the place is haunted. So what? I've seen worse from the carnies at the August Fair. I'm not letting this old bat scare us off. Now, come on."

Conner followed her closely behind like he was stuck to her with a strong glue, and this annoyed her to no end, but she decided not to call him on it. He was just a weenie, but he was all the help she was going to get, so that's all there was to it.

She shone her light into the kitchen, but there was no bust in there, obviously. Even so, the burners on all three metal stoves lit one after the other in timed procession. A slew of sharp knives stood up on their handles, their sharp blades suddenly pointing toward the ceiling.

It was unnerving to watch, but it was also infuriating. Now that Kara knew the place was haunted, these little antics were only further enraging her.

"That won't work on me!" she called out. "I'm going to find that diamond, you old bat! You're not stopping me!"

"Are you crazy!" squealed Conner. "Don't tick her off!"

"Oh, shut up, and let's go," said Kara unhappily. "I'm finding that bust, Conner. I want that diamond. I'm not going home without it."

"This is crazy!" whispered Conner. "We should get out of here!"

Kara ignored him and left the kitchen entrance. Conner followed her like a frightened puppy as she led him down yet another hallway. They shone their lights in what looked like a downstairs guest room, but there was no bust in that room, either.

"Nothing here," stated Kara. "What we need to find is the—"

She was cut short as the old woman in the black dress appeared right in front of her.

The old woman stepped from out of the shadows on Kara's right, but this time the phantom held an old cavalry saber in her withered right hand. The apparition swung the blade as Kara stepped backwards out of a fight or flight response, and the blade thunked into the wooden doorframe in front of them.

"Run!" yelled Kara.

She followed her own advice and bolted down the hallway, Conner following her, the young man shrieking like a little girl the entire way. They ducked into a large room at the end of the hall, and Conner slammed the door shut a second later.

"That was a real sword!" screeched Conner. "That was a real sword! It almost killed you!"

"Shut up!" hissed Kara. "I need a moment to think…"

She shone her light around the large room, and the ensuing glow revealed bookshelf after bookshelf stacked with books. There were several leather-backed comfy chairs scattered about, but the eyecatcher was the huge writing desk parked in front of some large glass doors that led outside.

The floor was grey marble, there were potted plants in white vases here and there, and there were even paintings of the founding fathers on the walls…The whole of it would have been a relaxing studious atmosphere were it not for the fact that they were being pursued by a murderous ghost in the pitch black of a haunted mansion on a stormy night.

"We're in the library," whispered Kara. "We've found the library…"

The circular glow of her flashlight came to rest upon a white terracotta bust, that bust positioned upon the impressively large desk in front of the outside doors.

Kara's smile widened to the point where she thought her lips would split her face in two, but her enthusiasm could not be contained over this discovery.

"There it is!" she said excitedly.

"What?" asked Conner meekly.

"The bust!" grinned Kara. "We found it!"

"You still want that stupid bust!" gasped Conner. "Are you nuts!"

"It's right there, you idiot!" hissed Kara as she motioned toward it with one open-palmed hand. "We'll unlock those glass doors and take it out that way! Now come on!"

"Why can't we just break it open here?" asked Conner. "Then we can grab something real fast and leave! Let's just break it open and get out of here!"

"And how are we going to do that?" asked Kara in irritation.

"We stand on that desk and drop it," said Conner. "The floor's marble, and the bust is terracotta. It's first grade."

Kara thought about this and then nodded in agreement. This was actually a good idea.

"Okay," she agreed. "But let's do this quickly before that old bat shows up again. This bust is her 'most prized possession,' after all."

"Right," said Conner.

The two made sure to unlock the glass doors before getting up onto the library desk. Once up and on the desk, they groaned and strained to lift the heavy bust of old Mr. Carter.

"This thing…is heavy!" panted Kara.

"Yeah…" groaned Conner.

"Now…you know…why I needed you!" she grunted.

They held the bust between them, an ugly thing of old Carter's shoulders and withered face, but no matter how ugly it was on the outside, the only thing that mattered was what was on the inside.

"Get ready…to toss it." panted Kara. "On three…One…two…"

The interior door to the library blew open as if pushed by a mighty wind. There, in the doorframe, stood the ghost of old Mrs. Carter, a ghastly green glow about her, her sable widow's dress flowing in a phantom breeze, a very real and deadly saber in her withered right hand.

Conner shrieked and pitched the bust early. The young man jumped from the desk and ran after that. He opened wide the glass doors behind the desk and ran into the raging storm outside, disappearing into the night.

Kara's attention, however, was elsewhere, and her fleeing partner in crime was the last thing on her mind.

Kara watched as time slowed in her vision. The bust fell toward the marble below, and though there was a furious apparition with a sword before her, and though her companion had fled like the weenie he was, all she could think about was the diamond she was about to gain. All she could think about were her fingers wrapped around that diamond, about the money she was going to make off of that diamond, about the beach she would be lounging on, piña colada in hand…Oh, yes. She was finally going to be rich.

The bust cracked apart as it struck the marble of the library floor, chunks of the bust skating across the slick marble in various directions.

Kara stared at the contents of the bust for a precious few seconds before full comprehension set in. Her eyes widened as she sucked in her breath in horror, and then she jumped off the desk and ran through the open doors and out into the stormy night.

There was the murderous ghost, the general atmosphere of the storm, and her inadequate partner in crime, and she could handle those things, but there was only so much she could take, so even her will broke, and she ran.

Inside the bust was no diamond, no. Inside the bust was the rotting skull of old Carter, what was left of the leathered flesh pulled tightly across yellowed bone and grinning teeth, empty sockets where eyes had once been, the ravages of time taken in its appropriate toll.

#3…BLACK JACK CROSSBONES

That painting's a killer work of art.

Tyler laid down in bed as his father tucked him in.

"Now, go to bed, young man," said his father. "I know we're in a new house, but there's no reason to be scared."

"I liked the old house better," said Tyler.

"You just turned four," said his father. "You're a big boy now. Sometimes, people have to move when times call for it. Your daddy has a better job, which means I can take you to more places…"

"Like the park?" asked Tyler.

"Yep," nodded his father. "Like the park. Now, get some sleep."

"But I'm scared," said Tyler.

His father sat down on the bed and gave him a deep look of concern.

"Scared of what?" sighed the man. "There's nothing to be scared of."

"I don't like the painting on the wall," said Tyler.

He was, of course, referring to the painting hanging just above his dresser. The previous owners of this house had left that painting behind, much to Tyler's misery.

The painting was of a large wooden ship, an old-timey thing called a "sloop," but that wasn't scary. It was the people on the ship that scared him, because they looked mean, as did their captain, a big man with a black beard and an eyepatch along with a funny black hat. This man looked to be the meanest of them all.

Even worse was the flag the ship had on its mast, because it was all black with a scary white skull-and-crossbones on it. Tyler did not like this flag at all. It made the painting look even scarier than it should have been.

"That painting?" asked his father as the man turned to stare at it. "That's not scary. It's just a pirate ship."

"I don't like the scary flag with the bones on it," said Tyler.

"That just means it's a pirate ship," said his father.

"I also don't like the man with the funny hat," said Tyler.

"That's just the pirate captain," said his father. "He's not scary…not unless you lived in the 1600s or…whenever pirates were around…It's just a painting, Tyler. It can't hurt you."

His father sighed and shook his head.

"Look…" said the man unhappily. "I know we took Mr. Woogums away from you because…because we thought it was time you didn't need him anymore…but maybe you need him tonight, huh? Maybe just for tonight?"

Tyler nodded in reply. He could really use Mr. Woogums right now.

"Okay," smiled his father. "I'll get Mr. Woogums."

His father stood up from the bed, walked to the closet, opened the closet door, and took Mr. Woogums from the top closet shelf, a place so high that Tyler could never ever reach it on his own. The man walked back to Tyler's bed, sat down, and handed Tyler the ratty, tattered, old teddy bear.

"Here's Mr. Woogums," said his father. "Now, this is just for tonight…and don't tell your momma. She'll have a fit if she finds out."

Tyler nodded in understanding. He was only four, but he wasn't stupid.

His father mussed Tyler's hair in affection, stood up from the bed, walked to the bedroom door, and flicked off the light. He stood in the doorway for a moment before smiling at Tyler one more time.

"Goodnight, champ," said the man, and then he was gone, the door closing behind him.

Tyler's nightlight flipped on. The dim glow of the little light revealed the painting on the wall again, but Tyler did not like this. He did not like the way the strange work of art was cloaked in striped shadow.

He tried to sleep, but the creaking of the bed prevented that. The bed itself rocked slowly from side to side, and darkness crawled in from every wall. He could hear the faint voices of others from somewhere above him, but that was impossible, because his room was on the second floor, and the only thing above him was the attic.

Tyler did not know what was happening, but he did not like it, so he clutched Mr. Woogums tightly and got down from his bed. His feet touched floorboards instead of soft carpet, and this made his little heart race. Things were only getting worse, and he feared that the scary painting was the cause of it all.

He took several steps upon creaking wood in the dark before he realized that his nightlight was out. There was a faint glow coming from the ceiling, little lines of light from above, but from where, he did not know.

He turned to look back toward his bed, but it was no longer there. In its place were the dark outlines of wooden barrels and crates, nothing more.

Tyler clutched Mr. Woogums and made his way to where he thought the bedroom door was. He reached up for the knob, but there was no knob, and in its place was a flat handle, so he pushed down upon it and pulled hard to open the door.

The door opened up to reveal a set of wooden stairs that led upwards. There should have been a carpeted hallway in front of him, the bathroom on his left, his parents' room on his right, but those rooms were no longer there.

Nevertheless, he took to the stairs, because he needed to know what was going on and where his mother and father were.

"Be careful," whispered Mr. Woogums. *"This is a bad place."*

Mr. Woogums sometimes talked to Tyler, but only when Tyler needed some encouragement. He had never actually warned Tyler that some place was bad before.

"I want Mommy and Daddy," said Tyler.

"They're not here right now," whispered Mr. Woogums. *"We need to go back."*

"Go back where?" asked Tyler.

"Go back to your bed," whispered Mr. Woogums.

"I still want Mommy and Daddy," said Tyler.

He reached the top of the stairs and discovered another door like the one he had just opened. He reached for the handle on the door, but he was stopped by yet another warning from his faithful teddy bear.

"Don't open that," warned Mr. Woogums. *"This is a bad place."*

"I want Mommy and Daddy," repeated Tyler.

Mr. Woogums simply did not understand this. The old tatty bear could not comprehend that only Tyler's mother and father could fix things.

Tyler pushed down on the handle and pulled open the door anyway. He stepped out into sunlight, which was odd, because it was supposed to be nighttime right now. He knew it was nighttime, because it had been dark outside, and he only went to bed when it was dark.

Tyler's eyes widened as he viewed his surroundings, because he was on a ship like the one in the painting. This old ship rocked back and forth due to the unsteady sea all around, and just like the painting, there were mean men everywhere, the mean men in the funny clothes with cloth hats on their heads.

"Hey!" cried one of the mean men as he grabbed Tyler by his little arm.

Tyler was too scared to even scream. He was dragged forward from the open doorway that led down into the ship's hold, the mean man dragging him forward so that all of the other mean men could see.

"Look what I found, lads!" yelled the man.

The other mean men surrounded them in a circle, all of them yelling and laughing and saying bad words, but they were not what froze Tyler stock still in his rocket pajamas. No, it was the meanest man of them all that stomped forward in cuffed leather boots that terrified him. The meanest man of them all, that mean man from the painting, stomped forward and glared down at him with one good eye.

This man wore a funny black hat with an upturned brim. He had a black eyepatch over his left eye, and he was dressed in a seaworn, dark-blue coat with wide cuffs around his thick wrists. He had a mean, mean face hidden behind a bushy black beard and mustache, and Tyler was frozen solid from terror just by looking at him. Tyler's father had called this man "Captain," so that's what he had to be.

"A stowaway!" yelled the captain. "A filthy little bilge rat eatin' up the stores!"

The mean men around Tyler yelled and laughed and said bad words, and this terrified Tyler, but there was nothing he could do.

"He be too small for a powder monkey, lads!" yelled the captain. "Throw him to the sharks!"

The mean men that were gathered in a circle grew deathly quiet at the captain's command. There was a black aura that had settled down upon them, something that Tyler could not form into words for a description in his own mind.

"But, Cap'n…" said the man holding Tyler's little arm. "He's just a little one…We could make him one of us…"

The captain stared this man down with his one good eye, his face a shrine of terrible fury.

"This ship be no nursery!" yelled the captain. "Are you a wetnurse, you fool! I said, throw him to the sharks!"

"But he be just a boy—" started the man that was holding Tyler's arm.

The captain, the meanest of them all, the man with one eye, a bushy beard, and a funny black hat, drew a strange-looking pistol from his belt and pulled the trigger in a flash of fiery gunpowder. The loud "BANG!" went off, and then the man holding Tyler's arm let go of Tyler as he pitched backwards to the floorboards below.

Tyler looked over to the man on the deck. This man stared up at the sunlit sky with wide sightless eyes, a look of surprise permanently etched upon his weathered face. There was a large hole in his dirty white shirt, and from that hole spurted blood, bright red in the sun.

The man was dead. Tyler knew what "dead" meant. That meant he was gone forever. Dead people got buried in the ground at the cemetery, and they were gone forever.

Tyler looked back up at the captain, but Tyler was still too frightened to move, so terrified that he could not so much as twitch a muscle.

The meanest man of all, the captain, raised his funny-looking pistol high and barked out a warning to the rest of the crew.

"I be Black Jack Crossbones!" yelled the captain. "I be the captain of this here *Deadly Dirge*! Is there any other scurvy seadog that be challenging me!"

A big man in a dirty striped shirt and baggy brown pants stepped forward and drew a sword that Tyler's father had called a "cutlass."

"You shouldn'a killed yer own, Cap'n," growled the big man in the dirty striped shirt. "Rogue or no, there's a law on the sea…so I be takin' over now."

The crew backed away in silence as the two men faced off against each other. The captain drew his own cutlass and leveled it at the big man in the dirty striped shirt.

"Mutinous dog!" yelled the captain. "I'll hang ye from the yardarm for the birds to pick at yer eyes!"

Tyler wanted to clutch Mr. Woogums out of fear, but the old tatty bear had gone missing. He looked down to his left at the body of the man with the hole in his chest, and Mr. Woogums was there, right there next to that man's still and lifeless form.

"Down here, Tyler," whispered Mr. Woogums. *"Look here."*

Tyler looked down at the funny-looking pistol resting across Mr. Woogums' lap. The old bear must have taken the thing from the dead man that had first accosted Tyler.

"Take it," whispered Mr. Woogums.

Tyler looked back up at the two men about to duel.

"I think I'll be takin' that hat," growled the man in the dirty striped shirt.

"The only thing you'll be takin' is a watery grave," growled the captain in return.

The two men went at each other a second later, but their duel was over in a flash. Their swords clanged against each other for a few brief hits, and then the captain backed away, drew a hatchet from his belt, and threw it with terrible force at the big man in the dirty striped shirt. The hatchet buried itself blade first right between the big man's eyes, and then blood sprayed everywhere as the big man fell backwards to the deck without a sound.

"Now, Tyler!" said Mr. Woogums with all urgency. *"Take the gun!"*

Tyler bent down and picked up the heavy pistol while the crew was fixated upon their own brutal captain.

"I be Black Jack Crossbones!" yelled the captain as he raised his cutlass high. "I be the captain of this here *Deadly Dirge*! Now, I say again…is there anyone else who wish to challenge me!"

"Shoot the captain, Tyler!" said Mr. Woogums. *"Point the gun at him and pull the trigger!"*

Tyler was not supposed to play with guns. His father had told him so. Nevertheless, he was scared beyond belief, so he raised the heavy pistol with both shaky hands and pointed it in the general direction of the captain.

"I be Black Jack Crossbones!" yelled the captain yet again. "I be the captain of this here *Deadly Dirge*! Now, throw this little bilge rat to the sharks! He's already cost ye two men!"

He turned to stare down at Tyler, his cutlass pointing in a straight line toward Tyler's little chest, his one good eye a flash of rage and fury.

That look of pure malice caused Tyler to jump, and his tiny fingers pulled backwards on the trigger. The gun went off in a flash of powder, a ball round shot from the barrel, and the force of it threw Tyler to the deck.

The shot went right through the captain's good eye and out the back of his evil head, leaving a small tunnel in its deadly wake. Tyler could see the sunny sky through that hole, the blue of it, and that surreal image burned itself into his brain.

The captain, the meanest man of them all, staggered backwards as the crew stepped aside for him. He pitched over the railing a second later, and then he was gone, gone forever under the rolling waves of the unforgiving sea.

"Now, run, Tyler!" cried Mr. Woogums.

Tyler did not even think to question his tattered old bear. He stood up, dropped the strange-looking gun, and ran back down the stairs from where he'd originally entered the deck, but in his haste, he left Mr. Woogums behind. There was no time to go back for the old bear.

Tyler ran back into the darkness of the hold, but his pajama feet-bottoms touched down on soft carpet once he reached the bottom of the stairs. He could not feel floorboards anymore.

He could see his bed in the warm glow of his nightlight, so he pulled himself up onto his bed and hid beneath the sheets. He let his tears flow as the horror of it all caught up to him, and he cried out as he clutched his pillow in fear.

The light flipped on a moment later, and Tyler looked up to see the bleary-eyed, sleep-ridden face of his father as the man entered the bedroom.

"What's going on in here?" asked his father.

Tyler sat up and wiped at his tears.

"I killed him!" cried Tyler. "I killed the mean man!"

"You did what?" asked his father.

The man sat down on Tyler's bed and wrapped his arms around him in a caring embrace. He held Tyler close and stroked the back of Tyler's little head to calm him down.

"Hey, hey, hey!" said Tyler's father in a soothing tone. "You just had a bad dream…It's all right, little buddy. It was just a bad dream…"

"The mean man wanted to…to throw me to the sharks…" wept Tyler.

"Throw you to the sharks?" asked his father. "You've been watching too much TV, little man…Look, look. It was just a bad dream. That's all it was. Everything's okay now. It's going to be all right…Why don't you tell me what happened, huh? Who's this mean man that wanted to throw you to the sharks?"

"The mean man from the painting," said Tyler in shaky breaths. "He killed the other two mean men, and he wanted to kill me too, but Mr. Woogums told me to pick up the gun, so I did, and I shot him…"

"You shot Mr. Woogums, or the mean man?" asked his father.

"The mean man from the painting," said Tyler. "I shot him, and he fell in the water."

"The mean man from the painting?" asked his father in slight confusion. "Do you mean the pirate captain?"

"Y…Yes," wept Tyler.

He didn't want to cry, but the memory of it, the horror of it, gripped him and would not let go.

"Oh, Tyler," sighed his father. "I told you…that's just a painting…I'll tell you what…Why don't I move that painting downstairs, okay?...Look, look…There are no pirates anymore. They were around a long, long time ago, but there aren't any pirates anymore…Besides, they don't even look that mean in the painting."

The man stood up from Tyler's bed and walked over to the painting.

"Even this pirate captain doesn't look…that…mean…" said Tyler's father as the man's voice trailed off in audible confusion.

Tyler looked up at what had caught his father's attention. There, in the painting, in the center of the ship, there was no pirate captain anymore. No, there was only the small painted image of Mr. Woogums, the tattered old bear in the center of the deck, a ring of pirates around him, their swords drawn and raised high, their faces lit with strange joy.

#4…WHAT'S UNDER THERE?

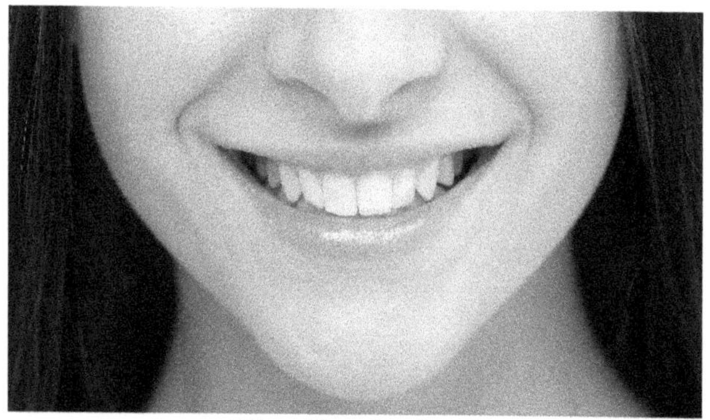

What IS under there?

Oliver walked into the kitchen and pulled on the hem of his mother's dress. The woman looked down at him and smiled, but he knew she was not happy he was in here.

"Yes, my little one?" she asked.

"Can I have a cookie?" asked Oliver.

"May I have a cookie," corrected his mother.

"May I have a cookie?" asked Oliver.

"You may, my little Ollie, but only one," said his mother as she held up her right index finger in front of his little face. "Dinner will be ready soon."

She ushered him over to the little square kitchen table and sat him in his booster chair. He was not a baby anymore, but he needed a little extra boost to properly reach his food.

The woman handed him his oatmeal cookie, and he held the big, round, edible disk in both hands. He took a bite of that delicious cookie, but there was a lot on his young mind, and he knew she could tell.

The older woman cocked her head to one side and looked down at him in strange concern. She smiled as she did so, an affect that Oliver was still not used to. His mother had never smiled so much until just recently.

"What is it, my little one?" she asked.

"When is Daddy coming home?" asked Oliver.

"Now, now," said his mother with a wagging finger. "Your father has gone away. He's not coming home."

"He isn't?" asked Oliver.

"No, no," smiled his mother. "We talked about this, my little Ollie. Your father's gone away, and he's not coming back."

He wanted to cry over this again, but he knew she would scold him if he did. She had told him the same thing yesterday, and he had cried then, and she had scolded him to the point where he had been terrified. It was something in her eyes that scared him so, and now he was too afraid to earn her ire again. Even so, his eyes watered at the thought of it, the thought of his father never returning home.

"Now, don't you cry," said his mother with a shake of her head. "Big boys don't cry…I know something that will help, though. I know exactly what you need. You need a glass of milk for your cookie."

He nodded his head in acceptance. He did not know why his father was not coming home, but he did not want to get in trouble anymore. Nevertheless, he saw something that bothered him, and it bothered him a lot. He couldn't help but ask about it.

"Mommy, why is your face peeling?" asked Oliver.

His mother's face was indeed peeling, peeling upon her left cheek, just a little, but enough to bother him, the pale skin off a tiny sliver, a fleck of jet black, like coal, beneath it.

"Don't you worry about that, my little Ollie," smiled his mother. "That's not important."

"Are you sick?" asked Oliver.

He had been wondering if she were ill, as she was not her usual self, and this bothered him…It bothered him a lot.

"Just eat your cookie, dearie," smiled his mother.

Oliver took a bite of his cookie, but it tasted funny. He had not noticed it with the first bite, but now he did. He hesitated to have any more, but his mother would not have it.

"Eat all of it," smiled his mother.

He took to eating the cookie again regardless of the taste. He did not want to get in trouble again.

"That's a good boy," smiled his mother.

She went to the fridge and pulled out the milk carton from it. She took down a glass from the left cabinet above the sink and poured him a tall glass of milk.

"Here you are now," she said as she handed him the glass.

He eagerly took the glass with both hands, as he was sorely in need of a drink, but the milk tasted funny as well, just like the cookie.

"This doesn't taste right," said Oliver. "The cookie doesn't taste right, either."

"You asked for a cookie, and you got one," said his mother. "I even poured you a glass of milk, Ollie. Now, don't be ungrateful."

His mother reached up and scratched at the left side of her face, and more of her skin peeled away, just a bit, but more than enough to make Oliver nervous.

"Mommy, why is your face peeling?" he asked again. "I don't like it…"

There were small scratches on her face where her nails had raked across her pale skin, and these scratches left strange lines of ebony, like black trails in peach-brushed snow.

"I told you not to ask that, Oliver," warned his mother.

She reached up and scratched at the skin of her left cheek again, and even more of her skin peeled away to reveal a small patch of pitch black beneath it.

Now Oliver really needed to know. He needed to know what was wrong with his mother, because something was wrong, very wrong, and he did not know what else to do but ask.

"Mommy, something's wrong with your face," he said nervously. "There's something under your skin. What's under there?"

His mother's eyes widened as she turned up her lips in a weird, disturbing smile.

"Do you want to know?" she asked. "Do you really want to know?"

In truth, Oliver did not want to know, because something was very, very wrong, and he was suddenly afraid to know. There was something wrong about everything right now, from his father not returning home yesterday to his mother acting all strange. Everything right now was wrong, so whether he liked it or not, he needed to know, so he nodded his little head in silent reply.

"Okay, my little Ollie," replied his mother. "I'll sing you a song about it…but you won't like it. You won't like it at all."

Ollie swallowed a chunk of cookie out of fearful reflex.

His mother stared at him with wide eyes as she sang with a smile.

"What's under there? What's under there?" she sang. "Under Mommy's face, so fine and fair? What's under there? What's under there? Under pale, pale skin and long black hair?"

She reached up and peeled off more of her cheek skin, revealing a large swatch of black beneath it, about the size of a thumb, and Oliver's little hands shook as he squeezed the half-eaten cookie in his clutching fingers.

"Daddy, Daddy, found a book," sang his mother. "He dug it out of a hidden nook. It told a lot of horrid things, written for the ancient kings. He said the words, he read them loud, and then sprang out a turbid cloud. Black and slick and old as ages, it billowed from the musty pages."

His mother continued to smile as she peeled off a large flap of pale skin from her left cheek. Beneath it were her teeth, the ivory pegs flawless in the light, but as she peeled backwards toward the end of her jaw, more teeth were revealed, all the same, but many more than there should have been, all the way back to the end of her jaw, all set in a line of ebony flesh beneath an outer layer of peeling, pale skin.

"What's under there? What's under there?" sang Oliver's mother. "Under Mommy's face, so fine and fair? What's under there? What's under there? Under pale, pale skin and long black hair?"

The cookie crumbled under Oliver's grip, the flecks falling like dust to the kitchen table. He shook in his chair, his mouth partially open, his eyes wide, his skin blanching as he continued to watch and listen to his mother.

"Ancient, ancient, billowed, and swirled, it sprang from the pages and into the world," sang his mother. "Existing long before Noah's Sea, antediluvian, finally free!"

It was something in her eyes that caused Oliver to shake, the madness and fury in his mother's eyes that held him in place in his booster chair.

"Daddy ran with all his heart, but he was quickly torn apart," sang his mother. "Mommy screamed and tried to shout, but she was eaten from the inside out!"

His mother tore off the pale skin from the entire left side of her face, the flap of it falling onto the floor in a wet plop of a white sheet, like rain-soaked paper.

The obsidian flesh beneath the peeling skin was slick and looked to be made of tiny overlapping scales. Her left eye was a golden color with a single, black, vertical slit where a normally-round pupil should have been, and a fire was burning within that black slit, but frosty-blue, like a flame made of ice.

Even her smile was uncanny, as the right side of her face held normal teeth and lips, while the left side of her face held a lipless mouth with teeth that spanned all the way back to her neckline.

"Now it's time for a little snack, made with fear in a fleshy sack," sang his mother. "Alive, alive, where you cannot move! That makes for a more delicious food!"

She finished her song with unusual gusto, the very sound of it echoing around the kitchen to assault Oliver's little ears without mercy.

Oliver's terror-induced paralysis finally broke as he willed his muscles to move. He hopped down from his booster seat and ran for the kitchen door, but the drug in his cookie and milk slowed him down far too much for him to actually make it there.

#5…THE LADDER IN THE TREE

She must find the courage to climb.

Eun-Yeong looked up at her mother and smiled.

"It is your birthday today, dear Eun-Yeong," said her mother. "You are turning thirteen, and that means you are becoming a woman."

"Yes, Mother," smiled Eun-Yeong.

"You are in charge of the house from now on," said her mother. "I am leaving, my child, and I am not returning. Do you understand?"

Eun-Yeong frowned and took in a short breath at this news, for she did not understand. She could not comprehend why her mother would leave her and not come back.

"Why are you leaving?" she asked. "Where are you going?...I want to come, too!"

Her mother placed her right index finger upon Eun-Yeong's lips and shushed her.

"You are a woman now," said Eun-Yeong's mother in a firm tone. "You will watch the house from now on. You will do the chores from now on. It is up to you to weave the cloth and take it into town for sale. It is up to you to buy supplies from now on. You will live here by yourself from now on…I am going to join your father."

Eun-Yeong was very upset about this. She did not want to live here by herself, nor did she wish to take care of the estate by herself.

"Where is father?" asked Eun-Yeong. "Why cannot he just return and help us? He left for the war, but he never came home. Do you know where he is?"

"I do," nodded her mother. "I promised him I would raise you until you became a woman, and now you have. Now, I must return to him, which means you now own our land. Do you understand?"

"No!" cried Eun-Yeong as she stamped her feet. "No, I do not understand!"

"It is about courage, dear child," said her mother. "Soldiers came to take your father away to war. Your father had the courage to tell them no, but he went with them anyway to keep them from burning down the house. He had the courage to go with those soldiers, and I have the courage to go to him, so you must have the courage to live on your own from now on. This is what your father and I have decided."

"I…" began Eun-Yeong, but she was at a loss for words.

"You are safe here," continued her mother. "The war is over. No one will come up here. You are safe here high on this cliff with the oaks overlooking the water. You must have the courage to live your life on your own."

"There are many things I cannot do on my own!" cried Eun-Yeong. "For instance, what will I do about the roof? You know I cannot climb! You know I cannot stand the height!"

Her mother reached down and touched Eun-Yeong's chest directly over her heart.

"You must find the courage to climb in here," said her mother. "If you must fix the roof, you must find the courage to do so…Now…I have wasted enough time on this. I have to leave, and you will stay here and learn what it means to have courage. You will not leave the house until tomorrow, and then you will be on your own. I am your mother, and you will honor my wishes."

Eun-Yeong was not happy about this, but she had to honor her mother's wishes.

"Yes, Mother," frowned Eun-Yeong.

She could not help but cry. It was not like her to spill tears, but the situation called for it.

"Dry your eyes, dear child," smiled her mother. "You will find the courage to live on your own…Now…you stay here, and I will be on my way."

Eun-Yeong nodded in acceptance, but she did not like this. It was not something she wanted at all.

"Go and work on the loom," said her mother. "You will lose your troubles in your work. You can prepare your own meals now, and you can manage the household on your own. You must find the courage to face the world alone, my child."

"Yes, Mother," sniffed Eun-Yeong.

She did as her mother had commanded. She went to work on the loom, and her mother took her leave.

Eun-Yeong worked on the loom until she was tired, and then she prepared herself an evening meal, though her thoughts were heavy on both the present and the future.

"What am I to do?" she asked herself. "How will I manage without Mother?...I must learn to have courage, or I will surely fail."

She slept on this thought as a storm brewed outside.

The next day, it was pouring, and the roof began to leak.

"This is what I was trying to tell her!" hissed Eun-Yeong in exasperation. "I cannot be responsible for everything! I cannot fix the roof!"

She thought of going into town to ask someone to help her with the roof, but she was afraid that someone would take advantage of her once they learned she was living alone. They might beat and rob her, take the house by force, or worse.

She set to catching water in buckets, placing them under the leaks, and then she went to work, weaving on the loom. Her mother was right about setting aside her troubles for work; it helped keep her mind off her fears.

Once she was finished with her work, she prepared her evening meal, ate, and then laid down for sleep. The storm was dying down, so the next day was a good day to work on overcoming her fears.

"I will find a way to fix the roof," she thought wearily. *"I must overcome my fears, and I will start with my fear of high places."*

The next day, the sun had come out in the morning, and she was ready to work on overcoming her fears. She walked outside to look up at the roof, but the height was still intimidating for her.

"I must overcome this fear!" she hissed. "I must find courage! I have to fix the roof!"

Her mother had taught her many things, even the knowledge of how to fix the roof, though she had never actually been up there.

"I will do this!" she said to herself. "I must!"

Eun-Yeong looked past the sprawling meadow outside the house. She looked out toward the row of oak trees growing on the side of the cliff they lived upon. There, leaning against the tallest oak, was their wooden ladder.

"That is what I will do," thought Eun-Yeong. *"I will start with that tree. If I can climb that ladder to the*

crook of that tree, then I can climb the ladder to the roof."

She walked across the meadow to the ladder in the tree and gripped its sturdy sides. She stepped upon the first rung and looked up, but the height made her dizzy, and she could not take another step.

"No, I cannot!" she thought. *"But I will not give up. I will try again later."*

She went back into the house and went back to work. She did her work, prepared her evening meal, and laid down for the night.

"I will climb the ladder tomorrow," she thought. *"I will do it this time. That tree looks out over the cliffside, over the ocean. I will climb it and look out over the ocean, and then I will know I can climb to the roof."*

The next day was as sunny as the day before. It was the perfect day for climbing the ladder in the tall oak tree.

Eun-Yeong took her leave of the house, walked across the meadow, and gripped the ladder with both hands.

"You must overcome your fears," she thought. *"You must have courage!"*

She stepped upon the first rung and looked up. The height made her dizzy, but she closed her eyes and took in a deep breath. She released her held breath, opened her eyes, and started to climb.

She made it about halfway up before she made the mistake of looking down. Looking down made her dizzy again, and she panicked. She clutched the ladder in terror before gathering the nerve to climb back down again.

"I will do it tomorrow," she said to herself. "I have the courage…I know it!"

She went back into the house after that, went to work, and took care of her nightly chores. She laid down for sleep after a long day, but the trial of the ladder in the tree was never far from her mind.

"I will find the courage to climb the ladder," she thought in defiance. *"I will look out over the ocean, and then I will have the courage I need to leave this place. I will go find Mother and Father, and then I will bring them home."*

The thought of this made her smile inside, and she rested easy that night.

The next day was cloudy, and Eun-Yeong knew more rain was coming.

"I must climb the ladder today," she said to herself. "I will climb the ladder and find my courage. Then I will fix the roof and leave to go find Mother and Father."

She gathered her courage, left the house, crossed the meadow, and made her way to the ladder in the tall oak tree. She gripped the sturdy wooden ladder with both hands, looked up, and started to climb.

She made it halfway up when she looked down again. The height made her dizzy, but this time, she steeled herself and shook her head no.

"No!" she said to herself. "I will climb the ladder! I will climb this tree! I must find my courage!"

She took in a deep breath, slowly released it, and climbed. She took one step after the other, and before she knew it, Eun-Yeong was at the top of the ladder and in the crook of the tree.

She held onto the branches as she looked out over the vast expanse that was the ocean, but there was something else that held her immediate attention.

Before her was a thick branch that stretched forth over the cliffside, over the crashing waves far below. It was impossible to see this side from the meadow, so its cliffside branches were only visible from the crook of the tree.

She had found her courage at the top of her climb, but she had also learned a terrible truth…She would not be leaving to find her mother and father.

Around that thick branch was a rope and a chain. Swinging from the rope was the rain-soaked body of her mother, the older woman's neck broken at an odd angle from the drop, her body swinging next to the chain-hanged, chain-bound, moldering skeleton of her father, his remains decayed and stripped of flesh by birds long, long ago.

#6…CORNERS

It's all peripheral.

Dr. Andrew Sidirov walked down the hallway to room 312. The patient in question was one Mr. Maximillian Davics, a former research assistant to the now deceased Professor Angus Macnally.

Andrew flipped through the chart on his clipboard for the times of the various medications his patients were taking. It was not yet time for Max's daily dosages, so now was the opportunity to talk more to the man before he was sedated again.

Two large and burly orderlies in crisp white clothing unlocked 312 for Andrew and let him into the unusual room. Room 312 was unusual in the fact that it was nicknamed the "Round Room," mainly for its sphere-like construction and the time it had taken to fit the necessary white safety padding within it. Max was simply too dangerous to be put in any other room, as this was the only room where he was nonviolent enough to be dealt with.

Andrew walked into Room 312 along with one of his orderlies for safe measure. The room itself had nothing in it but padding and a toilet, and even the toilet was padded.

He took out his tape recorder and pressed the record switch.

"August 27th, 1985," he stated. "Patient ID 159378686, Mr. Maximillian Alexander Davies. Caucasian, male, age 31, 5'10" in height, 183 lbs. in weight at last physical. The patient identifies himself as Max."

"That's right, that's right," said the man before them.

Max looked to be an ordinary man with a block for a face, black stubble swept across that block, that block of a face surrounded by short black hair that was slightly mussed. His dark eyes were wide and wild, an otherwise out-of-place feature for someone who could have passed for the neighborhood plumber. He was in white patient clothes, a short-sleeved shirt and pants, though he was not allowed socks or shoes.

"I'll be running the recorder for our session, Max," said Andrew. "Is that acceptable?"

"Oh…Oh, yes," said Max with an overly-emphasized, vigorous nod of his head. "Yes, yes. You'll hear them on the tape. You will…No…No, no…No, you shouldn't listen. You shouldn't hear them. That's bad. Don't listen to them. Don't hear them."

"Hear who, Max?" asked Andrew. "Who will I hear?"

"The Corner People," nodded Max. "That's what I call them, because they have no name."

"Who are the Corner People, Max?" asked Andrew. "Why don't you tell me about them?"

"They come at you diagonally," nodded Max. "They…They come out of the corners. You can see them out of the corners of your eyes. You can't see them when you look straight at them. That's how I keep them away. I look at the corners before they can get me."

"I see," replied Andrew. "Let me ask you a question first, Max…Can you tell me why you're here?"

"It's because of the professor," nodded Max. "It's because I was there when it happened."

"Why don't you tell me what happened, Max?" asked Andrew. "Describe it for me."

"No, no," said Max as he shook his head in vehement denial. "*Noooo*. No, I can't do that."

"Why not, Max?" asked Andrew.

"That's what they want," said Max quietly. "They want me to confess, but…but I have nothing to confess. I didn't kill the professor."

"We know you didn't kill the professor, Max," said Andrew. "His cause of death was listed as a single gunshot wound to the head. The coroner has determined that Professor Macnally's death was a suicide…Do you know why the professor would want to kill himself, Max? Any ideas?"

"He…He…He…" stammered Max.

"Take your time, Max," said Andrew in a soothing tone.

"He found out about them," nodded Max. "The professor knew all kinds of things about their kind."

"So do you, Max, don't you?" asked Andrew. "You were his research assistant. You should know what he was working on."

"Yes, yes," said Max quickly. "I was helping him with his research...with…with the artifacts he was studying."

"Artifacts?" asked Andrew.

"Yes," nodded Max. "Stone and fragments from before the Sumerians. They worshipped old, old gods back then. Gods long before the time of man. Gods from…from back before there was light."

"I see," said Andrew. "So, we've established what the professor was researching, but that doesn't explain his suicide. Can you enlighten me on why he may have killed himself? That information will help me help you, Max."

"No, no," said Max with a shake of his head. "No. You don't see. You don't see at all."

"What should I see, then, Max?" asked Andrew.

"You shouldn't," said Max as he shook his head yet again, this time with much more emphasis. "No, no, you shouldn't. Once you see them, they won't leave you alone. They hide in the corners, you know. That's where they live. They wait for you to see them, and that's when they strike…You can't let them in. You can't let them get inside."

"What happens if they get inside, Max?" asked Andrew. "What happens then?"

"They take over," nodded Max in strange understanding.

"I think, Max, that we should start an increase in your dosage," said Andrew. "That should prevent you from seeing these 'Corner People.' Then, after we've carefully measured your progress, we'll see about moving you to a more comfortable room. One with more amenities."

Max's quiet demeanor turned on a dime. His face twisted in both panic and rage as he shook his head in defiance.

"No," said Max angrily. "No, I'm not leaving. I'm not leaving here…You can't make me! I'm not leaving here!"

He rushed Andrew, but he did not make it to him. Andrew's orderly, a big and burly man a full head taller than Max, stepped forward to block the aggressive patient's hostile advance. They struggled as Max screamed and shouted in rage, though his babbling was incoherent, incomprehensible.

Andrew stepped out of the Round Room as the other orderly rushed in to block the door. There was screaming and shouting from within from Max, but that brief moment of enraged insanity was stopped as the orderlies stepped from the room and locked the door behind them.

Andrew flipped through his clipboard in order to review what increases in dosage he was going to have to give his seriously disturbed and unstable patient.

"I definitely think an increase to his anti-psychotic is in order," he muttered. "Obviously, I didn't bring a pen. I'll change the dosage in my office."

"Oh, I'll get that for you, Doc," said one of the orderlies, the one that had entered the Round Room with him.

"Get what?" asked Andrew in slight confusion.

"Oh, I have a pen," said the orderly.

He patted his back pockets but found nothing.

"I thought I had it…" he said uncertainly.

He stared at Andrew in confusion, but the only thing on Andrew's mind at that moment was panic.

"You brought a pen into the room with him!" barked Andrew. "Unlock the door! Immediately!"

He turned to view the port window to the Round Room, and there was Max, silent but smiling, holding up the ballpoint as if it were his ultimate prize.

"Max, no!" yelled Andrew, but it was too late.

Andrew's disturbed and mentally unstable patient plunged the ballpoint into his own left carotid artery with his right hand. Blood spurted in a crimson fountain across the pristine white of the Round Room, and Max stumbled backwards to fall to the padded floor below.

Andrew directed his two orderlies as quickly as he could.

"You, get on the phone and send the emergency staff here!" he roared. "You, get that door open now!"

The orderlies rushed to complete his commands, but Andrew already knew it was too late to do anything about this severe error in judgement.

✱✱✱✱✱

Andrew sat down at his desk in his study and released a long sigh. The day had not gone by quickly, and he wanted to lay blame for the horrendous incident at the hospital upon someone else, but he knew the tragedy was entirely his own fault.

He needed to go over Max's last words for a variety of different reasons, legal being at the forefront, but he was not looking forward to it.

He studied the timesheet in front of him, picked up his handheld recorder, and rewound the device to the correct time in question.

"What was going on in your mind, Max?" he asked himself. "Why did you and the professor kill yourselves, hmm? If only you could tell me…"

He pressed play on his recorder in order to listen to his brief and violent interview with Maximillian.

"August 27th, 1985," said his voice on the recorder. "Patient ID 159378686, Mr. Maximillian Alexander Davies. Caucasian, male, age 31, 5'10" in height, 183 lbs. in weight at last physical. The patient identifies himself as Max."

"That's right, that's right," came Max's voice.

"I'll be running the recorder for our session, Max," said Andrew's voice. "Is that acceptable?"

"He told you you'd hear us on the tape," came Max's guttural, whispered voice. "You didn't listen, did you, Doctor? He told you not to listen, Doctor. He said so."

The hairs on the back of Andrew's neck stood on end. This was not part of the interview, though he was certain Max had somehow altered the recording during their session, but how, he could not fathom. Andrew had been holding the recorder the entire time. There was no possible way he could think of as to how Max could have gotten ahold of the device.

"Hear who, Max?" came Andrew's voice over the tape. "Who will I hear?"

"We're coming, Doctor," came Max's voice. "We're coming for you."

The lights in the study flickered as Andrew looked around in sudden fear. That fear gripped his heart like a vice, but he would not give in to it. He would not become one of his own patients, mired in delusions and imaginary thinking.

"Who are the Corner People, Max?" asked Andrew's voice over the tape. "Why don't you tell me about them?"

"We see you, Doctor," said Max over the tape. "We all see you now."

Andrew immediately hit the stop button and shuddered uncontrollably in his seat. He closed his eyes, took in a deep breath, and pulled his wits back together to calm himself.

"It's all in your imagination, Andrew," he whispered to himself. "You're tired, and you're letting your imagination run wild. Don't become one of your patients. You know better."

He took in another deep breath, released it, and opened his eyes.

"There's no way Max could have recorded anything like that," he said with a grim smile. "Don't give in to sleep-deprived hallucinations. He never once had my recorder. There's no possible way Max could have done that."

Andrew nodded once to himself in determination and then hit play on his recorder.

"Max is dead," said Max's voice over the recorder. "Who do you think you're talking to, Doctor?"

Andrew hit stop on the recorder as the lights in the study flickered and dimmed. His hands trembled as he set down the recorder upon his desk and pushed it away.

"This is ridiculous," he said in a shaky voice. "There's no such thing as the Corner People."

The lights dimmed further but did not go out. He heard a whispering around him, low at first, a sibilant muttering at the back of his mind, and then the voices picked up, unintelligible, a language that should have never been uttered by anyone.

He could see the dark corner of his study on his south and west walls, the shadowy edge at the top of his room, and then two pinpoints of crimson light appeared, watching, like eyes fixed upon him. He snapped his head to stare into that pitch black of the corner, but there was nothing there.

"Ridiculous…" he choked out.

The whispering grew louder as he struggled to ignore it, but he could see the red pinpoints on the other side of the room within the dark recesses of the top north and west walls, but this time, he refused to look.

"There is no such thing as the Corner People," he said in a shaky voice. "There is no such thing…"

The whispering was deafening in his head as it threatened to overwhelm him. The pinpoints of red light in the north and west wall corner grew larger, more piercing, but he would not give in to delusions and madness.

"No…" he choked out. "I will not…give in…There is…no…such…thing…"

His shrill, high-pitched scream echoed round the study as a bony, ebony shape with red eyes and long black claws leapt out from the dark corner, leaping out toward him with a loud screech of its own, its gangly arms stretching forth, its knobby hands ready to grasp and rake with elongated fingers.

*****

Andrew whistled a tune as he walked the corridor of the hospital, his medication chart and tape recorder in hand. He was headed to room 201, but the patient in question was quite harmless, and she had been for some time now.

He stopped in front of her room and motioned for his two orderlies to step back.

"Alice is not a threat," he told the two burly men. "She has had episodes of sporadic tantrums in the past, but these have ceased within the last four months. Nevertheless, I'd like you two to wait outside the door in case I need you. I believe I can handle her on my own, but I'll call you in if I need any help."

"Sure thing, Doc," said one of the large orderlies.

Andrew nodded once as the other orderly unlocked the door for him. He stepped inside and hit the record switch on his tape recorder as the door shut behind him.

"August 28th, 1985," he stated into the device. "Patient ID 159378597, Miss Alice Elizabeth Lourdes. Caucasian, female, age 23, 5'4" in height, 111 lbs. in weight at last physical. The patient identifies herself as Alice."

The young woman before him sat on her bed and stared up at him with eager and interested eyes.

"I'll be recording you today, Alice," smiled Andrew. "I take it you have no issue with that?...I ask this every time, but you know I'm required to ask you, right?"

"Yes, Doctor," nodded the young woman. "I know...I'm doing everything I'm supposed to do. I'm better now...I am. I just wanted to say that I'm...I'm doing much better now."

"I know, Alice," smiled Andrew. "You've been taking less of your medication as recommended, and you've improved quite dramatically. However, I think further steps need to be taken."

The young woman's thin face wilted in visible disappointment over this news.

"Further steps?" she asked. "I thought I was doing better. I thought I was going to get out soon."

"Oh, no, dear," grinned Andrew as he shook his head in denial. "Oh, I think you'll be here for a good long while…"

Alice's eyes widened in sudden fear, her mouth dropping open in a silent gasp as Andrew stepped forward, his own eyes glowing with two bright pinpoints of crimson light.

#7…THE RED CANDLE

Don't light it.

Denetor waited in the lineup with the other acolytes. Their initiation was about to begin, and they would soon be full-fledged priests of the Seven Lights. Only acolytes were allowed into the recesses of the temple this time of year, that time just before harvest, that time when the guiding spirits were summoned and released into the land for the good will and fortune for all.

"This is the final step of your journey into manhood," said Old Garren as he walked the line, or rather, creaked slowly forward with the help of the knotted staff he leaned heavily upon. "With the summoning of the six, you will…"

"Why doesn't he just die already?" thought Denetor in irritation. *"He's older than my grandfather. There are far better to replace him."*

"The candles represent the best in man," droned on Garren, "and each of you will be given the color we think will serve you best. Though there are six to be lit, the seventh shall not be lit, as the refusal to light the seventh also represents the best in man, the tolerance, sympathy, and character of the righteous…"

Denetor stared over at Pallan, who stood at the end of the line. He glared at the young man with unrestrained hate, as Pallan was the favorite of the elders, a clear indication that the old priests were feeble-minded in their age.

"He stares ahead with that ignorant look of complacency," thought Denetor with a mental scowl. *"Bah! He's like a ram waiting to be slaughtered, but he's too stupid to figure it out. What a fool."*

"Now, you shall each receive your gift," wheezed Old Garren. "The young acolytes of the Makers will bestow upon you your candle, and this will complete their journey into womanhood as you complete your…"

"Womanhood?" thought Denetor. *"This is a pleasant surprise. We were told nothing about this ritual before coming in here. I did not know there would be women to serve us. Interesting…"*

"You will journey through the halls and follow the signs according to the color of your candle," droned on Garren. "Once you have reached your altar, you will light your candle and perform the summoning as practiced. The seventh candle shall not be lit, and the bearer of this candle shall receive special instructions, of which, you have not yet been taught. We do not teach this to acolytes for fear of…"

Denetor could not help but grimace and scowl over at Pallan again. The young man at the end of the line was always showing him up, was always ahead of him in one thing or another, and was always, *always*, receiving the praise of the elders.

"You deserve nothing," thought Denetor in silent rage. *"And nothing is what you will get. I will become the head of the elders…and once I am the archelder, I will decide what is right and what is wrong, not you, Pallan, you insignificant bug…I will be the archelder one day. That is my destiny to fulfill!"*

"And now enter the acolytes of the Makers," wheezed old Garren. "They create the candles of the Seven Lights, they endanger their own lives for the creation of our people's hope, and they…"

"Ah, enter the women," thought Denetor with a grim smile. *"Show me which one is mine. She is most certainly finer than anything Pallan will receive…"*

The young women entered in a line procession and stood before them.

Denetor carefully studied the young woman before him, as each of these young acolytes of the Makers was approximately the same age as they were, around sixteen or so cycles grown.

Denetor's acolyte was a young woman of a somewhat-plain nature in the face, with long brown hair done up in a bun in the back, that hair held up by a Maker's wooden wreath. She held in her soft, pale hands a plain white candle, nothing particularly special.

He looked at his six other companions' candle bearers, and each of them was of varying quality with varying colors for their candles.

Eto's woman had light-brown hair and was short like Eto, but she was cute in the face and held a light-blue candle between her short fingers. Dannas' woman was a tall, attractive strawberry-blonde with a golden candle, Murket's woman was a raven-haired beauty with a lavender candle, Ollos' woman was a short, squat, and cute brunette with a spring-green candle, and Jomachus' woman was very pretty, with sandy-blonde hair and a silver candle.

Denetor saved Pallan's inspection for last, because Pallan's woman was surely like Denetor's, plain and bare of quality.

Pallan's woman was a tall and stunningly-beautiful platinum blonde, gorgeous in every aspect, and in her soft hands, she bore a tall and imposing blood-red candle, the largest and most striking of the gifts presented to them.

Denetor inwardly bristled at this brazen insult. It was clear that the elders thought nothing of him. Worse yet, they thought he *was* nothing, but this insult would not go unpunished.

"Now receive your candle, young acolytes of the Seven Lights," stated Old Garren, "and your journey shall begin."

The plain young woman before Denetor stepped forward and proffered her candle to him.

"Receive the Candle of Mercy, oh bearer of purity," she said in a practiced tone.

Denetor took his candle, but he was careful not to show his rage. He would deal with this situation as warranted in his own way, and he would do so quickly.

"You may now enter the Halls of Spirit," called out Garren. "Follow the colors of your candle to your altar, light your candle, and perform the summoning. In each chamber, an offering shall be made, save for the seventh chamber, where only the unlit candle is placed. The offerings are presented on a dais next to the altar of your chamber. In your chamber, your spirit assigned to you, one of the seven spirits of the hearts of men, shall speak to you, and the land shall receive its blessing."

Denetor took one last look at Pallan, but he was further enraged as Old Garren took the young man aside and spoke to him in private. It was clear that Pallan was receiving even more favor, and this…this could not, *would not*, go unpunished.

"I will teach him a final lesson," thought Denetor in grim determination. *"That is my destiny."*

He followed the other acolytes into the Halls of Spirit, all save Pallan, who was still with Garren. Denetor waited for the others to pick the hall with the corresponding colors of their candles, and they each took to their designated routes, but Denetor did not enter the white hall. No, he had other plans in mind.

He entered the hall with the blood-red stonework and walked down its narrow corridor. There were torches in sconces on each side of the hall to light the way, so he made his way to the altar chamber with little difficulty.

Within the small chamber was a large flat altar of blood-red stone, and behind it was a huge, ornate, metalwork throne of wrought black iron, the iron twisted to look like daggers, knives, swords, axes, and clubs of varying lengths. There were two lit braziers filled with incense and woodchips, those braziers smoldering away on each side of the throne, their smoke lingering upwards towards open chutes in the stonework.

On his immediate right was a dais, and upon it was a long, curved, and wicked-looking dagger with a bejeweled golden handle.

"Humph," snorted Denetor. "They serve him something more befitting a man, while mine is surely only fit for a child…No matter. I will see justice done."

He gave himself a grim smile as he took the dagger from the dais, replaced it with his white candle, and waited next to the entrance of the altar room. He then pressed flat against the blood-red wall so that he could not be readily seen.

It was not long before Pallan entered the room. The smug, arrogant young man walked into the center of the small room and looked over at the dais in noticeable confusion. It was clear the old man had told him about the dagger.

"What is—?" was all he had a chance to say.

Denetor leapt upon him with all the speed of a ravenous wolf. He plunged the curved blade into Pallan's back, and he did not stop stabbing even after Pallan lay unmoving and lifeless upon the floor in a pool of his own blood. Denetor stabbed and stabbed due to years of pent-up rage, years spent within this pretender's shadow.

Denetor stood and tossed the bloody dagger aside. His tunic and face and arms and legs were splattered with blood, but he didn't care. He held the red candle in his hands, his prize that was his and his alone.

"Now, I will take what is mine," he said angrily.

He lit the blood-red candle by means of the brazier on his left and placed the lit candle upon the altar. A deafening quiet descended upon the room like a shroud, and this spooked him, but only for a moment. He held firmly to his resolve and spoke the words of summoning, because it was his destiny to do so.

"I summon the spirit of this candle so that the hearts of men may receive its blessing!" he said loudly, his arms raised high. "Show thyself, oh, Spirit! Come forth and bestow your blessing!"

The braziers flickered and burned low as a chill descended upon the altar room. Denetor backed away toward the entrance as he was struck with a sudden unnamable fear.

A crimson light picked up around the throne of black metal as a form began to take shape, and then the braziers went out altogether. There was only darkness now, an unnatural darkness lit by the scarlet glow around the throne.

The spirit sitting in the throne took shape and stood.

Denetor released a chill gasp as his visible breath entered the frosty air around him. His dark hair turned white upon viewing the specter before him, and he had no words or thoughts escape his ice-locked mind. Nothing escaped his lips but a shrill whine to show for his foolishness.

The spirit was a nude, emaciated, and gaunt figure of ghastly quality, headless with a stump for a neck, its skin a rotted grey and brown, and it held up its right arm as if holding a lantern with no light. In its rotted skeletal right hand was a long rusty loop of chain, that chain attached to its own rotting skull by wrought black-iron bolts inserted within each side of the bone. Those bolts were buried in each side of this spirit's rotting skull, the skull's pate missing, as if a sharp blade had taken off the top part of its bodiless head.

The foul spirit reached forth with its left hand, picked up the lit red candle, and placed it within its own skull as if the rotted braincase were a special holder meant just for that. The candle's eerie light shown through the orbital bone sockets, and the rotted skull's jaw creaked open to speak in a terrible, dusty voice devoid of care or sympathy.

"The offering is accepted," it said, its terrible voice booming round the small chamber. "Let the Spirit of Murder enter the hearts of men."

The spirit twisted into a blood-rose of light and flew forward, flying straight through Denetor, leaving a roaring within its wake. It disappeared through the entrance of the small chamber and vanished altogether.

Denetor dropped to his knees and held his head in his hands. He took in several short and panicked breaths before dropping his hands to the floor to support his weight.

He stared at his hands, his hands resting within the pool of Pallan's blood, and a plan began to form within his young mind.

Normally, there was no way to fix this, but he was not about to give up…This wasn't his fault anyway. This was all Pallan's fault, but he knew a way to fix it.

First, though, he would pay a visit to the plain young woman that had been his candle bearer, the one that had handed him the worthless white candle.

He stood, walked over to the discarded dagger, and picked it up with his bloody right hand. He stared longingly at it as he put forth a grim, determined smile.

Yes…He knew exactly what to do.

#8…THE TIMING IS MINE

There's no love lost here.

Sally hurried back to the house as quickly as she could. That pathetic, sniveling younger sister of hers, Alice, was planning something disastrous, and Sally was determined to put a stop to it.

"She's probably gotten ahold of the last of Daddy's money," she thought. *"Well, we'll see about THAT."*

Their father had passed away not more than a month ago, but the old fool had gotten into more than enough trouble with his creditors, and now the bank had taken almost everything. But Sally knew that the paranoid old man had stashed away some of his cash somewhere within the old mansion, and dollars to donuts, Alice had found it.

Alice had always been the studious one, always reading this and that while picking up new skills. She had taught herself to quilt, had taught herself first aid, and had even taught herself how to fix a car, but it was her philanthropy that ground into Sally. That whiney, irritating, little do-gooder was a thorn in her side, almost as big a thorn as Constance.

Constance was more like Sally, so she was definitely a bigger problem, but Sally's older sister was also shortsighted. That woman didn't know her hat from a banker's check, so she had probably never even thought of Daddy stashing away any sizable amount of money.

"I can't let that money go to waste," said Sally to herself. "Constance wouldn't hand over a penny, and Alice would probably donate it all to sick orphans or some such nonsense. There's no way I'm handing over that cash to either one of them. Not one single cent."

She pulled up to the old mansion drive in her Studebaker, but her instincts had proven correct. There was her younger sister, Alice, leaving the house, locking the door behind her, and in her altruistic little hands was a large leather handbag.

"You little…" hissed Sally.

Alice deposited her skinny self into her own Crosley station wagon, and the middle-aged woman was off, probably to spend every last penny of the last of the family fortune on some unforgivably-wasteful charity.

Alice pulled out and past Sally's Studebaker, and their eyes met. The look of panic on Alice's face told Sally everything she needed to know.

"Traitor!" yelled Sally, even though she knew Alice could not hear her from within the confines of the Studebaker. "You vagabond! That's my money!"

Alice backed out with such haste that she almost hit the opposite side of the road, nearly ending up in the northside ditch.

Sally flipped her own gear in reverse and pushed hard on the clutch to follow her.

"Come back here!" shouted Sally, the sound echoing throughout her car.

Alice backed out into the road just as another car pulled up behind her. It was Constance's own Muntz, the one Daddy had bought her with money he hadn't had to spend, but this posed yet another problem, for Constance was in the race now.

"Not that parasite!" hissed Sally.

She shifted into first, hit the gas, shifted into second, and was in hot pursuit of her younger sister a second later, her older sister right behind them both.

"That's my money!" yelled Sally as she rolled down her driver's-side window.

She hit the gas on their back road as all three cars headed toward town, a dangerous race that Sally was determined to win.

Sally sped forward as she drove up next to Alice in the driver's lane, Alice's Crosley in the passing lane, and as fortune would have it, Alice's front passenger window was down.

"Pull over!" yelled Sally, her face hot with rage. "Pull over that piece of junk right now, Alice!"

Alice shook her head no in silent defiance, her face a picture of sheer panic. Sally's younger sister hit the gas and sped forward, and Sally was honestly surprised that the little do-gooder had it in herself to defy Sally's well-deserved rage.

"That little, pathetic, whiney…!" hissed Sally as she raced to catch the last of their family's fortune.

Constance's Muntz sped past her in the passing lane, and Sally let forth a series of expletives that would have made a sailor proud.

The three cars hit the city limit in nothing flat. Alice's Crosley slowed down as she turned onto Main Street, Constance following her closely behind, with Sally trailing a not-so-distant third.

Sally followed both cars down Main until Alice pulled up and parked in the lot of the Parkerdale Commerce Bank.

Sally swore yet another litany of curses as she realized what Alice was going to do.

"Oh, no, you don't!" screeched Sally.

Handing over the last of Daddy's money to those vultures at the bank was even worse than wasting it on charity. There was definitely no way Sally was going to put up with that.

She pulled up the Studebaker beside Constance's Muntz and blocked her older sister from opening her own car door. It would take that parasite a moment to get out through the passenger side, and that was all the time Sally needed to claim that money.

Alice exited her own Crosley and made a run for the bank, but the middle-aged woman was not so spry anymore, and she fell hard to the pavement, the large leather bag sliding out of her pathetic, slender little hands.

Sally dropped her purse in the front seat, grabbed her keys, and was out of her Studebaker in a flash. She clutched her keys in her left hand as she ran across the lot towards her one and only goal.

She was on the bag in a heartbeat. She picked it up and clutched it closely to her chest in triumph.

"No, you can't take that!" screeched Alice.

"I'll take what's rightfully mine, you little fool!" hissed Sally. "You're lucky I don't kick you while you're down!"

Alice burst into tears as she tried unsuccessfully to stand. Her elbows and knees were skinned, and her green-print dress was torn, so she wouldn't be putting up any kind of a fight.

"They took everything!" wept Alice. "You can't take that! Justice is all I have left! They stole everything! You don't understand! I have to give it to them! I have to get to the bank! There isn't any time left! You have to give it back! You don't understand!"

"I understand you're a weak little fool!" yelled Sally. "Go back to your books, you pathetic little worm! Teach yourself how to grow a spine!"

Sally started back toward her own car, but she stopped stock still as she stared into the determined face of her older sister, Constance, and more importantly, Constance's Muntz. That parasite had pulled back and out from her parking space and was now revving the engine of her overpriced vehicle in what was clearly an attempt to commit vehicular murder.

"You wouldn't da—" whispered Sally, but the forward motion of the Muntz cut short that sentence.

Sally danced backwards as she turned to run. She dashed toward the sidewalk as Constance hit the gas in an attempt to run her over. Sally barely made it to the walk, but she fell to her bottom as Constance slammed on the breaks just before the grill would have turned Sally's face into mush.

"Ha!" mocked Sally as she struggled to stand. "I knew you didn't have it in you!"

She got to her feet just as Constance exited her car and chased after her.

"Come back here, you lush!" yelled her older sister.

Sally stumbled and ran as Constance pursued her.

"I won't let you waste it all on men and booze!" screeched Constance.

"You'd just gamble it all away, you hypocrite!" yelled Sally in return.

Sally ran down the walk as her older sister ran after her. She made it halfway down Main before Constance tackled her from behind. They both stumbled and fell, and then they were rolling around on the pavement in front of the post office as they attempted to wrestle the bag out of each other's hands.

"It's mine!" cried Constance. "Give it to me! Daddy left that for me!"

Sally managed to get to a standing position as the two fought over the bag, but her parasitic older sister would not let go of the prize between them.

"It's mine!" yelled Sally. "You can rot in the poorhouse, you thief!"

"It's mine!" screeched Constance. "It's my turn, and it's my time!"

"The timing is mine!" shouted Sally in return.

She took to hitting her older sister with the keys in her left fist as she clutched her prize with her right. She hit Constance twice in the face before the older woman fell to the pavement while holding her bloodied right cheek.

The prize was Sally's, and the timing was indeed hers. She sneered down at Constance and then gave her a nasty little smirk.

"You'll never be anything but a lowly little peasant," she gloated in triumph.

Constance stood and staggered toward her, but Sally knew the gambling thief would no longer be any trouble. The fight was out of her older sister, and if it wasn't, Sally was not above finishing her off.

Sally pried open the leather bag and studied its contents with both hunger and the pride of victory.

"It's all mi—" was all she got to say.

The alarm clock within the bag rang as the timer ran out. The crude clock mechanism Alice had pieced together had served its purpose, and the dynamite attached to it exploded, destroying a chunk of the post office parking lot while damaging a small portion of Main Street.

#9…THE CALLOUS ONES

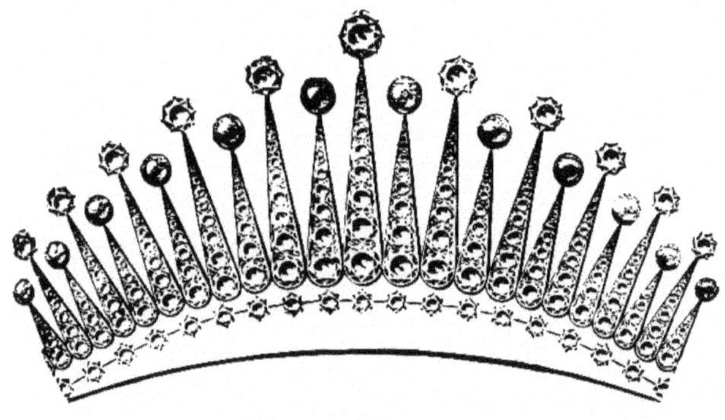

There will be blood.

Roren stared up at his master, the Great Sage, Althar. They were in the Grand Hall of the Imperial Palace, and many, many people were gathered here. It was due to the fact that Emperor Thardon was dead, assassinated in his bed while he lay asleep.

Roren's master had already warned him that there would be blood, as the rulers of various city-states and provinces were all gathered in one room, and that was always a recipe for disaster.

"Stay close to me, boy," warned Althar as he gave Roren a knowing gaze. "You will not want to be away from my protection once the fighting starts."

"Yes, Master," replied Roren.

It was true Roren was only ten cycles old, but he was a good and studious apprentice, and he was not stupid, so he would do as his master commanded.

Roren's master had taken him under his wing two cycles ago, as Althar was getting old, his long white beard and wrinkled face a testament to the old man's age.

Althar was not titled the Great Sage for nothing, for he held much knowledge within his wizened mind, from the lost tomes of Atalantia to the ethereal texts of the Astral Expanse, so he knew things that others did not, hidden, arcane secrets locked away by time and ruin. He had advised many kings before there was an emperor, and he had even advised the previous emperor, Emperor Thardon's father.

With all of his master's knowledge and accomplishments, Roren was proud to be Althar's apprentice.

But Roren did not have long to ponder his master's significance before he was forced to follow the Great Sage to the bottom of the steps at the base of the empty Imperial Throne.

Master Althar tapped his knotted oak staff upon the white marble of the palace floor. His knocking attracted everyone's attention, and suddenly, all eyes were upon the Great Sage and his young apprentice.

"If you know anything of our glorious empire," stated Althar, "then you know who I am. As the Emperor's most trusted advisor, he warned me that there would be an attempt on his life. Unfortunately, he was correct. Emperor Thardon has been slain."

There came an immediate uproar as nobles and knights alike vied for attention. It did not take long, however, for Roren's master to quell their panic and anger.

The old sage thumped his staff once upon the white marble, the stone plate beneath that wooden rod cracked, and a blast of wind blew through and over the gathered crowd.

"Silence!" cried Althar. "There is more to this than I have yet stated!"

Roren was in awe at how the crowd hushed in response to his master's powerful presence. He knew now more than ever that he wanted to follow in Althar's great footsteps. There was no doubt about this in his young mind, nor would there ever be.

"Each of you seeks to take the throne," said Althar in a warning tone, "yet none of you seek the responsibility of such a position of power. There will be a reckoning for the murder of the emperor, but the assassin is still among us…Yes…the Callous Ones have returned."

There was an immediate uptake in angst amongst the crowd, but at a lower decibel than their previous uproar. Yes, Roren was only ten cycles old, but he could sense their nervousness and fear as if it were a shroud worn upon them all.

"As you know," stated Althar, "the Callous Ones brought despair and ruin to the land one thousand years ago, and it was not until the last of them had been driven out did we finally have some sense of peace."

Roren knew the story of the Callous Ones. They were the old sorcerers that had made a pact with the Old Gods, and they had been stripped of their emotions, stripped of any sense of mercy, charity, or goodwill for their bargain, but they had been given power, real power, and that power was not something anyone could ignore.

"How is it that you have proof of this!" called out the beautiful blonde regent of Larmond.

"He has no proof!" cried Red Saber, the pirate lord.

"When was the last time anyone heard of the Callous Ones!" yelled the knight captain of the Order of Wander.

"The Callous Ones are a myth!" yelled the fat king of Aranol. "Such things do not exist!"

"They do exist!" barked Althar in return. "And you shall listen!"

His visible rage silenced every leader without further warning. Roren was impressed at how his master could discipline both nobles and commoners alike with but one warning glare. The Great Sage was truly great.

"The Callous Ones have returned!" yelled Althar. "You are all in danger as long as they defile our land!...But that is not the worst of it! The worst of it is something that no one wishes to believe!...Their leader, the Evil One, has returned!"

The gathered nobility exploded in angry shouts and verbal rage at this development, but Roren knew his master could, and would, handle them. These people were like scared sheep, but his master was the shepherd, and he would keep them under control.

"Silence!" shouted Althar as he slammed his staff upon the marble floor.

The nobility, the kings and queens and knights and gentry of their land, settled into a reluctant silence once more.

"I have warned you that a reckoning is coming!" cried Althar. "Only the strongest amongst us may take the throne!...The Evil One has returned and is one of us! The Evil One has slain the emperor and is here right now, here within these very walls!"

Althar switched his staff from his left hand to his right and laid his left hand upon Roren's right shoulder, pulling Roren backwards and closer to him. Roren knew right then that things were about to get bad.

"What are you speaking of?" asked the knight captain of the Order of Wander. "What would you have us believe?"

"He's saying that one of you is the Evil One, you self-righteous fool!" yelled the fat king of Aranol. "Not that your failed order could protect this empire, so you would do well to silence your fool mouth...

"Tis clear your order is a shallow front for your own thievery! You've gathered far too much coin for ones so dedicated to 'justice and honor.' Everyone knows your ilk charge for your so-called 'protection.' You count one coin after the next for deeds that should be done in good faith... Your swords are only drawn if you hear the clink of a jangling purse!"

The knights of the Order of Wander drew their blades, as did their captain.

"Tis a bold statement from a little man with too much meat," growled the knight captain. "You plunder your own kingdom for vanity's sake, yet you offer nothing to your people but cruelty and starvation. They cry to you for mercy while they cry to us for justice! Our kingdom's border is overwhelmed with the scabs fallen from your wounds…

"Dying refugees lace our walls, yet we cannot grant them sanctuary because of the plagues they bring with them, plagues you should have contained and healed, plagues caused by the breadth of your noxious opulence! You disgust me, you overstuffed pig!"

The king of Aranol's guards drew their blades in response to this unrestrained insult, but it was the noblewoman of Larmond that briefly prevented them from shedding blood, though her response did not help or resolve their row in the slightest.

"How can you fight amongst yourselves!" cried the regent of Larmond.

The tall, nobly-dressed woman raised her bejeweled staff high and then pointed it at the pirate lord, Red Saber.

"Can you not see a villain when one stands before you!" she called out. "This dog has raided our coasts for years, and yet nothing has been done to put him down! He has plundered our villages and ravished our women with impunity, yet our cries for justice have always fallen upon deaf ears...

"We have no navy to bring him to his knees! The emperor did nothing as this dog led a pack of vicious hounds into our borders to maul and defile my people, young men slaughtered like lambs in the streets, young women dragged away by their hair…This beast is the Evil One! He should be executed immediately, and if no one will do this justice, then I will!"

The pirate lord brandished his saber as six of his most trusted men pulled forth their swords and knives.

"You'll be taking that back, you speckled harlot!" he shouted. "We all know the tales of your debauchery and murder! Seven young lads and seven young maids from across your holds comes to your chamber on the Eve of Old Hallow, and seven young lads and seven young maids disappear with nary a trace the next day, never to be seen again…

"Oh, yes, old hag. We all know the secret of your youth…Sacrifice and blood be your reign. Even the most practiced knave looks like a saint compared to the likes of you!...It be clear who had a grief against the emperor, and it be clear who the Evil One truly be!"

"Dog!" screeched the regent of Larmond in unbridled rage. "You'll die for that!"

"Yes!" shouted the king of Aranol. "Death is on the table tonight!"

"So be it, tyrant!" shouted back the captain of the Order of Wander.

"Death it is, then," said Red Saber with a cold grin.

Roren was shoved even further backwards by his master as the room erupted in blood and violence.

The fat king of Aranol drew his ceremonial blade as his guards and the knights of the Order of Wander commenced in battle. The royal guards of Aranol, however, were far from ceremonial, deadly in their prowess, so the battle between the two groups was by no means uneven.

On the other side of the room, a different battle was waging. The regent of Larmond waved her staff once, and two pirates of the Broken Sea burst into flames, screaming as they staggered and fell as living pyres. The regent's guards took advantage of this momentary horror, and they engaged the remaining pirates, including Red Saber.

Roren clutched Master Althar's white robe in temporary shock, but this would not be the last horrific scene to be set before him.

Noble lords and ladies alike, unaffiliated with the four groups, ran in desperate cries and panicked screams as they trampled one another to reach the exit doors to the Grand Hall of the Imperial Palace.

Roren watched in stunned silence as an aged noblewoman had her skull crushed into bloody mush under the stamping boots of four different people.

Roren could not move as he viewed the terrifying, bloody scene playing out before him. He had known it was going to get bad, but the reality of it was far more than he could actually handle.

The knights of the Order of Wander fell one by one as the royal guards of Aranol fell with them, a bloody battle of slashing blades and no mercy, but Roren could not look away. He was transfixed by the gory violence, a paralysis of shaking hands and widened eyes.

All of the knights of the Order of Wander were dead moments later, save for the knight captain, and all of the royal guards of Aranol were dead, save one, but he was gravely injured with a stab wound to his chest. All of the dead within the two groups had limbs missing, mortal stab wounds, or heads rolling across the marbled floor.

The knight captain ran through the fat king of Aranol, ran him through his fat belly with a keen-edged longsword, and then the last of the Order was stabbed in the back by the dying royal guard, the sharp blade puncturing through both sides of the captain's breastplate to protrude from his chest, the deadly tip soaked in gore.

All of them were dead now, unmoving, never to breathe again, but Roren had no time to process this. No, he could only turn his head to view the last remnants of the other battle.

The pirates were all dead, as were the regent's two guards, and it was just Red Saber and the regent left, though the pirate lord held his bloody left side with his left hand as he dueled the regent, saber to staff, in a whirlwind of brutal fury.

Their weapons connected several times before the duel abruptly ended. The regent of Larmond swung her staff in a wide arc, the bejeweled tip crackling with orange magical energies, but the terrible weapon never connected. Red Saber ducked under her overswing and stabbed her through the stomach. She bent over as her mouth opened in surprise to spit out a line of blood, and then the pirate lord withdrew his blade from her guts and cut off the noblewoman's head with one swing.

The head of the regent of Larmond rolled across the marble floor to land at Roren's feet, and he stared down at the beautiful face of the older woman, that face resting between his leather shoes. He picked up her head without thinking, his young mind far and away from the brutal reality around him.

She held a permanent look of surprise upon her beautiful face, her ruby lips parted in an 'O,' her blue eyes wide with shock. Her long blonde hair trailed behind her head in a ponytail held up by her bejeweled silver tiara, the tip of her golden locks just brushing the floor below.

Roren let out a low gasp as the head he held in his hands withered and pitted into a grey, mottled husk, its shape aging in rapid succession of year after year, deteriorating in a span of seconds until it slipped through his small fingers as ashen dust. That dust spilled around the hem of his robe and his leather shoes, the silver tiara clanking to the marble beneath him as it rolled away across the slick floor.

The room reeked of blood, offal, and corpse dust as Roren tried not to gag in both disgust and horror. The nobility had all fled, and only Althar, Roren, and Red Saber remained, the dead their only company in the opulent Grand Hall.

The pirate lord stared up at them as he staggered forward, his pocked and weathered face spiraling out with black lines, a sure sign of some virulent poison or foul curse that had afflicted him.

"The witch…got me…" he choked out as he fell to his knees.

His dark eyes locked upon Roren and his master, and then those two hardened orbs stared directly into the face of the Great Sage. The pirate lord nodded once and put forth one last grim smile as he leaned upon his bloody saber for support.

"I see now…" he said, bloody spittle running down his bearded chin. "Well played…"

He fell dead to the white marble after that, and Roren allowed himself to take in one shaky breath upon watching him fall.

Roren released his breath and then addressed his master. The bloody fighting had shaken him to his knees, but he still had his master, and Althar was all the protection he would ever need.

Roren gathered his wits, but his little hands still shook as he tugged upon the Great Sage's white robe.

Althar turned and stared down at him, a look of unusual calm upon the old sage's face.

"Is the Evil One dead now?" asked Roren. "Some of the people ran. Did the Evil One get away?"

"No, child," said Althar in odd serenity. "The Evil One is not dead, though some obnoxious and ambitious threats were disposed of."

Roren's heart skipped a beat as he tried to process this.

"The Evil One got away?" he asked.

Althar shook his head no and gave him a strange, unnerving smile.

"No, my little apprentice," he said firmly. "The emperor died a natural death in his sleep, and his heir is yet to be chosen. With no heir, the land will fall into chaos, and it is my duty to see that it does not. You see, my child, the Callous Ones are long dead. They've returned only in the story I have told. In the same respect, the Evil One is not dead, because the Evil One is only a story. There was never any Evil One."

#10...RADIATION IS NOT OUR FRIEND

Time for the ol' class fieldtrip.

"Take your seat, James," said Ms. Hatcher. "You have a very special role today. Do you remember where your seat is?"

"Yes, Ms. Hatcher," said Jimmy. "Mine is the easiest to remember."

"That's right, James," said Ms. Hatcher. "Now, take your seat."

Today was an exciting day for him, and for everyone else, for that matter. They were finally beginning their fieldtrip to the Yard, a day long in the making. As his friends and fellow classmates boarded the bus right along with him, Jimmy was just happy he didn't have to sit through another boring class. He liked the fun stuff anyway.

"Everyone, take your seats!" called out Ms. Hatcher. "If you can't remember your assigned seat, just ask me!"

They all piled in and took to their assigned positions.

Jimmy took his seat in the back, and it was a special seat, something he was very proud of. Fifth grade was tough enough without special duties, but Jimmy had never and would never complain about his assigned role. Ms. Hatcher saw something in him that was great, and he was proud of that.

"Now, I want everyone to thank Mr. Jackson for driving us today," said Ms. Hatcher. "He's very, very good at his job, so he deserves our special thanks."

"Thank you, Mr. Jackson!" said all of the kids at the same time, including Jimmy.

The older man smiled, took off his dark-blue bus-driver's cap, and wiped the dark skin of his brow before putting his cap back on his balding head.

"You kids hold tight now!" he said in excitement. "We are going to have some real fun today!"

"Yaaaaay!" cheered everyone, and even Ms. Hatcher clapped in return.

Ms. Hatcher clutched one of the two poles at the front of the bus as the vehicle powered up.

"Now, everyone, be sure to pay extra-special attention to all instructions today!" she said firmly. "You've all practiced and practiced for just this day, and now this day is here, so you all know what to do! You have to listen to me and Mr. Jackson whenever we give orders!"

"Yes, Ms. Hatcher!" said everyone.

The thick lead and steel wall that comprised the exit to the compound rolled upwards as red lights swirled in warning on the garage ceiling. A klaxon blared as the compound door opened to its maximum height, and the bus rolled out into blazing daylight.

"In the old days, school buses used to be yellow," explained Ms. Hatcher, "but as you know, that color changed to varying gray splotches. Does anyone know what the color of our bus is called?"

Donny Bueller raised his hand in tentative reply.

"Yes, Donovon?" asked Ms. Hatcher.

"Camouflage?" replied Donny.

"Yes," nodded Ms. Hatcher. "Does anyone know what type of camouflage?"

Sarah Holiday raised her hand, and Ms. Hatcher nodded her head in response.

"Urban camouflage," said Sarah confidently.

"That's right!" smiled Ms. Hatcher. "Camouflage gives the bus some visible protection from attack. We call it 'urban' because we live in the city, so it's city camouflage. We learned to use camouflage by observing wildlife that used natural coloring to hide from predators…when we had natural wildlife, that is."

Jimmy checked his seat monitor to view the black and white images outside. There was nothing, really, but burnt-out buildings, old blackened vehicles, and debris here and there. The streets were relatively clear of obstacles, though. The Engineering Corps had done a good job of moving junk and whatnot off the roads, though that job was extremely dangerous.

"Now, once we're past the red line," said Ms. Hatcher, "we'll go into red alert mode. You have to watch your screens for that. Once we're in red alert mode, I want you all to remember your assigned tasks, okay?"

"Yes, Ms. Hatcher!" said everyone.

Jimmy was brimming with excitement, and he could tell everyone else was, too. Everyone had been practicing hard for this day, and this was more like a test than a fieldtrip anyway. It was time to show off what they could all do.

He looked over at Madison Taylor, the only other student assigned to one of the "special seats." She smiled over at him and nodded once in understanding. They were both going to be busy once the bus crossed the red line, so they were comrades in arms for the day.

It did not take long to reach downtown, though it felt like an eternity.

Jimmy braced himself as the bus neared its first checkpoint.

"Here we go, kids!" said Mr. Jackson. "Everybody, hold on and get ready!"

Red lights flashed on the bus ceiling as they crossed the red line on the satellite map.

"Now, class!" cried Ms. Hatcher. "Take positions!"

Jimmy smiled and nodded once to Madison, and she smiled and nodded once back to him. They both hit their elevation buttons at the same time, the lead and steel ceiling panels above them slid open, and their seats slowly rose upwards until they were in their assigned positions within the ball turrets on the roof.

Jimmy grasped the large handles of the flame gun within his ten-year-old hands. He watched the monitor in front of him for any and all threats, and he knew Madison was doing the same. The other students were on the side guns and/or threat location, though they were not as exposed as Jimmy and Madison were.

"Here they come!" said Mr. Jackson over the crackle of the intercom. "We've got dogs at nine o'clock! Ball gunners, we've got vultures coming in from five o'clock!"

"That's your side, James!" came Ms. Hatcher's voice.

Jimmy watched the screen in front of him as dark shapes flew out of half of what used to be a high-rise. The grotesque birds were each as large as a fourth grader, and each of them had razor-sharp talons and twisted corkscrew beaks with spines along their ugly, featherless necks.

Jimmy swiveled his turret, flipped on the gas switch, and then hit the ignition trigger as he doused the leading birds of the flock with white-hot flame. The burning mutations slammed into the street behind them as

Madison roasted more of them upon the passing of the flock overhead.

The rest of the flock scattered after that, survival taking priority over food in their twisted, chaotic instincts.

Emaciated, furless mutant dogs with oversized fangs dashed into the street to eat the corpses of the burning buzzards.

Jimmy's eyes widened at the sight of them. He'd studied the various types of mutants, but only in class, and he'd only fought them via simulation. Real life was much more exciting and much more dangerous.

He checked the Geiger counter next to his monitor, and it indicated 100 microSieverts. It ticked up to 115 in a matter of seconds, then 135, then 165, so they were nearing a hot zone, and that reading was just the interior of the bus.

He couldn't imagine what it was like outside, probably two or three full Sieverts, enough to fry him to a crispy critter. He was suddenly glad he'd had his dose of nano-bond this morning, because even the interior of the bus was starting to get dangerous, at least for an exposed length of time.

His attention was snapped back to reality as Mr. Jackson's voice called out over the intercom.

"This is where it gets dangerous, kids!" he said. "Hold on!"

"We're entering a humo-zone!" said Ms. Hatcher. "Everybody, stay on alert! Mr. Jackson may have to run through barriers, so prepare for impact! Don't worry about the bus; that's what the reinforced cowcatcher is for, but mutant attacks might still penetrate our shielding, so we need preemptive strikes before any attacks can reach us."

Jimmy silently thanked the heavens that their bus was camouflaged, or they would have never made it this far. The mutant creatures out there could spot color differences from miles away, even through all of the burnt-out buildings in the way.

Ms. Hatcher continued to teach as the bus sped along through downtown. Her voice was loud and clear over the coms, even with the overlapping crackle of radioactive interference.

"As you've learned in class, humos have human DNA," she explained. "They're much more intelligent than the other mutated life, and they have been known to use primitive weapons alongside their natural attacks. However, their most dangerous feature is the ability to look human at times, but make no mistake, they are *not* human, and they must be eliminated like any other mutated animal. Does everyone understand?"

"Yes, Ms. Hatcher!" replied the class into their coms, including Jimmy.

"Now, everyone, get ready!" called out Ms. Hatcher. "The first barrier is coming up!"

"Here we go!" cried Mr. Jackson a second later.

The bus shook as a loud crash hit Jimmy's ears. He checked the monitor to see chunks of concrete and brick scatter along the sides of the bus, wreckage of what was left of a crude humo-barrier they'd just crashed through.

Loud dings and thumps hit the sides of the bus as thrown objects were flung at them.

Jimmy checked the monitor to see humos appearing from out of makeshift shelters here and there, and some of them were truly grotesque. Some of the humos had multiple arms or legs, some were covered in boils, some had weird, malformed limbs, and some had weird, elongated limbs, but they all looked vaguely human, which was disturbing in itself.

Jimmy checked the fuel for his flamer. It was at 90%, but there was no reason to blast anything until he absolutely had to, and that was in spite of the fact that he was both excited and afraid.

"Humos at ten o'clock!" called out Mr. Jackson. "Humos at three o'clock, too! We're about to hit another barrier, kids! Brace for impact!"

Jimmy knew that the guns on each side of the bus were busy repelling boarders. He knew this, but it still surprised him when a humo landed on the roof right in front of his camera.

Mr. Jackson plowed through the next barrier, but this one had been connected to some kind of metal and stone tower, and that construct tumbled in pieces across the top of the bus. Along with it had come an intruder, and that intruder was what held Jimmy's attention for the moment.

The young teen girl on the camera looked to be about twelve or thirteen, a little older than Jimmy, but her face was beautiful, though smudged with dirt. She had bright eyes, though what color, Jimmy couldn't tell because of the black-and-white monitor, but she had an angelic face, one that radiated purity beneath her mop of short dark hair. She wore the basic rags that most humos wore, but this did not deter from her inherent beauty.

She reached forward and touched the camera with one extended, normal-looking human finger.

Jimmy wondered if she were some sort of captive, but he also wondered how she could survive at all in such outside conditions. The Geiger counter next to the monitor read 600 microSieverts, and that was just inside the bus.

Time seemed to slow as the young teen girl looked at the camera with bright, longing eyes, probably bright-blue eyes, eyes that stared right through Jimmy's screen and into his soul. It was the expression upon her beautiful face that ate at him; it was one of terrible want and hopelessness, and that combination was something that wormed its way straight into Jimmy's heart.

He was snapped from his hesitation and mental lack of wherewithal by the firm, calm, and instructive voice of his teacher.

"You've got a boarder, James!" stated Ms. Hatcher over the com.

Jimmy watched with wide eyes as the girl on the screen transformed. Her beautiful face split down the middle to reveal a huge maw filled with circles of spiny teeth, and dark tentacles slithered out from that maw right toward the camera.

Jimmy flipped the charge switch and electrified the outer rim of the ball turret. The humo-girl popped off the back of the bus, sparks surrounding her, and Jimmy hit the ignition switch on the flamer. The girl lit up like an ancient Christmas tree, and then she was rolling in a wreath of flame upon cracked pavement a moment later.

"Good job, James!" encouraged Ms. Hatcher over the com.

Jimmy shook his head to get himself back on track. He would have to talk to Ms. Hatcher later about the interaction; they really needed to add something like this to the simulation runs at the compound. He was lucky, however, to have had a nonlethal encounter with a humo, and because of that experience, he would not be taken in by another one of their tricks.

But good news was already on the way.

"We're through, kids!" called out Mr. Jackson. "It's smooth sailing to the Yard from here!"

There was a loud cheer over the com as the whole class celebrated.

Jimmy smiled and breathed out a sigh of relief. He was still wired, but he felt really good, regardless.

"We are off alert," said Mr. Jackson. "I repeat, we are off alert."

"Everyone can relax for now," said Ms. Hatcher. "It's only five minutes to the Yard."

Jimmy hit the elevation button and waited as he was lowered from the ball turret position. He sat back and smiled over at Madison as soon as he was back in the passenger position.

"Wasn't that awesome!" asked Madison in a hushed breath.

"Yeah," nodded Jimmy. "It was just like the simulation…Well, almost like it."

"I know," grinned Madison. "It was intense. It's going to be even more awesome when we get to the Yard, though."

"Yeah," replied Jimmy. "I'm ready for the next level."

They both relaxed as the bus neared its destination, both of them enjoying a few quiet minutes to reflect on their overwhelmingly successful run. It was not long, however, before Ms. Hatcher announced their arrival at the Yard.

"Okay, class," said Ms. Hatcher. "We're almost to the Yard. As you know, this is both a fieldtrip and a transfer. Once we're at the Yard, you'll head in with me and be assigned to a new teacher…"

There were immediate cries of protest and disbelief from the entire class. Jimmy had suspected that Ms. Hatcher would be leaving them, but he hadn't wanted to believe it.

"Hush!" called out Ms. Hatcher. "Hush, now! You all knew this day would come! We'll get you assigned to your new rooms, and then you'll each be going into your fields of expertise. You won't have just one teacher anymore. You'll have at least three or more from now on. You're becoming adults, and this is what's expected of adults…"

There were even more cries of protest and a few groans of despair.

"Everything's going to be fine," explained Ms. Hatcher. "You're all going to have a lot of fun without me. It's time for me to teach a new class with new kids…Don't worry…It's not the end of the world…again…Anyway…Anyway, class, the Yard is coming up, so I want all eyes on your monitors…All eyes to the monitors, class!"

Jimmy turned his eyes upon his own monitor. The Yard was coming into view, and it was much more intimidating than he'd ever suspected.

Thousands upon thousands upon thousands of charred, blackened skeletons and bones were heaped up on each side of the street. There were so many that Jimmy thought his eyes would pop out of his head upon viewing them.

"It is estimated that around 96% of the world population died during the first few years of World War III," said Ms. Hatcher. "That means only 4% of the world's populace survived, not including humos. For example, if one hundred people were fleeing a burning building, then only four would have escaped the fire."

Jimmy had heard this lecture before, but the enormity of those numbers still escaped him. All he had ever known was the compound, so he could not imagine what the world would have been like living outside with all of those people before the Great War.

"The Yard is where our city disposed of most of the city's dead," said Ms. Hatcher. "For some reason or another, the humos avoid this place, which is why our adult training facility is located here, otherwise known as Compound A. You were all living in Compound C, the children's crèche. You'll learn about Compound B, the strategic-resources facility, once you graduate your adult training.

"Anyway, you'll be living in Compound A from now on. Now you get to live in a bigger space with better training and more advanced equipment."

Jimmy thought about this, but he still didn't like the idea of losing Ms. Hatcher to another class. It bothered him a lot.

But Ms. Hatcher seemed to know what was on his mind.

"I know I'm leaving you, class," she said in a sad tone, "but I wanted you to know that these last few years have been wonderful, and I'm so proud of you all. Thank you all for doing your absolute best. I'm going to miss every single one of you."

Jimmy could just see the glint of a tear in her eye, even from the back of the bus.

"Let's not be sad now!" smiled Ms. Hatcher. "Let's not be sad! Let's finish the trip with a song instead. We all know which one to sing, don't we?"

And they did. This was a no-brainer.

They all picked up in song as Ms. Hatcher led the first verse. Jimmy sang loud and clear alongside Madison, because even though they were losing their teacher, they were gaining a bright future.

"Raaaaadiation is not our friend!" sang the class. "Raaaaadiation is not our frie…end! We'll kill anything that it might send, 'cause raaaaadiation is not our friend!"

About the Author

Mr. Marlott has a background in psychology and classic literature, and he enjoys literature of all types and genres. Mr. Marlott lives somewhere within the United States, has two Gen-Z children, and enjoys telling stories to anyone who will listen.

Books and Sites

You can read new stories of mine for free at bloodytwine.com. This site is my workshop where I work on new stories and perfect them for publication.

If you want the basic building blocks to writing genre fiction, you can explore my two cents on the subject in *The Quick and Easy Guide to Writing Genre Fiction*.

For great cosmic horror, you can read some awesome eldritch-horror tales by Bert S. Lechner. You can purchase Mr. Lechner's collection of cosmic horror, *The Roots Grow into the Earth*, wherever it is sold. You can also check out Mr. Lechner's personal website at bertwriteshorror.com.

For a mix of traditional horror and cosmic horror, check out some incredible short stories by James Dermond. You can purchase Mr. Dermond's *Doorways to the Unseen* series wherever it is sold. You can also visit Mr. Dermond's website at jamesdermond.com.

If you like this book, give it a good review and tell me what your favorite story was in this bundle.

THE QUICK AND EASY GUIDE TO WRITING GENRE FICTION

Thinking of writing your own tale of love, redemption, and heroics? Writing genre fiction is an art, and *The Quick and Easy Guide to Writing Genre Fiction* provides the building blocks for being successful in this art. Learn all of the necessary techniques to get yourself started with writing in your chosen genre. Whether you're writing a mystery, a romance, a thriller, science-fiction, horror, fantasy, or any other genre, you'll have the foundation for writing great stories right here at your fingertips in this guide.

Included in this guide is a step-by-step instruction of what it takes to put together your creation in any genre. Also included in this guide is the complete creation process of an original short story by author Matthew L. Marlott, so you, too, can have an easy example of how to create your own stories, whether those stories are short stories, novels, or novellas. You'll be able to create your own worlds and your own universes, so learn the basics of writing genre fiction for the purpose of selling, for publication on a site, for fanfiction, or just for your own personal satisfaction.

Remember, if you want real life, you can just walk out the front door. Why not write down your own story on paper or screen instead? Get started with your journey into genre fiction by learning from this invaluable guide. Don't wait until you're on your deathbed. Get started today.

Matthew L. Marlott

THE ROOTS GROW INTO THE EARTH

"In the dark we found them…"

The Roots grow into the Earth. Unseen conduits of Power, growing through the darkness of the void; walkways for malevolent, eldritch things to travel, connecting their dead worlds to ours.

In this collection of nine short stories and novelettes, you will find tales of unfathomable predators, cosmic gods, dark magic, and the people who cross their path: from archaeologists, long on the search for the find of the century, ensnared by a being beyond their understanding, to a man who notices a detail on a wall in his house for the first time, unwittingly inviting the attention of a malefic force from beyond the stars.

The Roots Grow Into the Earth consists of nine of Bert S. Lechner's previously published works, including three stories available as standalone eBooks: Interstate, the Wall, and Joanne's Vault.

Bert S. Lechner

DOORWAYS TO THE UNSEEN

"The Doorways to the Unseen series is a collection of short story books from author James Dermond. The stories take the reader around the world and through time, with each tale offering a glimpse into a supernatural episode. Every volume in the series contains six short horror stories meant to chill the blood and inspire unimaginable terror in their readers.

"So, step inside and find that which has been hidden from you all along. Where the unknown and the unimaginable meet."

James Dermond

Until Next Time…

Bloody Twine #1
Twisted Tales with Twisted Endings
Copyright 1st ed. © 2023 Matthew L. Marlott